Immediate Family

Immediate Family

Ashley Nelson Levy

FARRAR, STRAUS AND GIROUX

NEW YORK

·

Farrar, Straus and Giroux
120 Broadway, New York 10271

Copyright © 2021 by Ashley Nelson Levy
All rights reserved
Printed in the United States of America
First edition, 2021

Hand-lettering by Thomas Colligan

Library of Congress Cataloging-in-Publication Data
Names: Levy, Ashley Nelson, 1985– author.
Title: Immediate family / Ashley Nelson Levy.
Description: First edition. | New York : Farrar, Straus and Giroux, 2021
Identifiers: LCCN 2021008603 | ISBN 9780374601416 (hardcover)
Subjects: LCSH: Brothers and sisters—Fiction. | Adopted children—
Fiction. | Families—Fiction. | Domestic fiction.
Classification: LCC PS3612.E936747 I66 2021 | DDC 813/.6—dc23
LC record available at https://lccn.loc.gov/2021008603

Designed by Abby Kagan

Our books may be purchased in bulk for promotional, educational, or business
use. Please contact your local bookseller or the Macmillan Corporate and
Premium Sales Department at 1-800-221-7945, extension 5442, or by email at
MacmillanSpecialMarkets@macmillan.com.

www.fsgbooks.com
www.twitter.com/fsgbooks · www.facebook.com/fsgbooks

1 3 5 7 9 10 8 6 4 2

For my parents and my brother
And for D

That was a memorable day to me, for it made great changes in me. But, it is the same with any life. Imagine one selected day struck out of it, and think how different its course would have been. Pause you who read this, and think for a moment of the long chain of iron or gold, of thorns or flowers, that would never have bound you, but for the formation of the first link on one memorable day.

—CHARLES DICKENS, *Great Expectations*

Immediate Family

L AST NIGHT I told you that today might be hard for us, and you said why, and I said because you'll be married and all grown up, and you said I'm already grown up, and gave me a look that I've never seen on any face but yours, a kind of mischievous pride that wavers between the certainty of your own truths and the question of whether you'll get away with them.

I was supposed to be with our mother, helping fuss over the bride, your soon-to-be wife, but instead I made my way over to your corner of the Mexican restaurant during the rehearsal dinner. Over your head was a red piñata and behind you was a large dark window that a few hours before had held the beach. You were surrounded by our father's friends, holding a beer that was as much a display item as the piñata; what you probably wanted was just an ice-cold Coke. The other hand was in your pocket and you hunched a bit in your collared shirt, happy to be noticed, to be at the center somehow, but unsure how to handle your body as a result. A month ago you had called to ask if I would give you a speech. When I saw your name I wondered if you were calling to apologize, to set things right between us, but instead you cut right to the question. This is exactly the way you said it: *Will you give me a speech.*

I listened closely to the sound of your voice because I didn't hear it as often these days, and rather than being upset like I'd thought, I marveled at the feeling it brought along, like no time had actually passed, like the bad things hadn't happened or maybe they still had and regardless here we were, back to our old selves again. A speech? I said. Isn't that a best-man thing? And you explained that your best man had backed out of the speech, maybe even backed out of the wedding, and you didn't want to talk about it because it was a long story and please. You said please twice, please give the speech, you were in a bind. Otherwise would you really be asking your sister?

Did Mom put you up to this? I said, and you breathed a loud sigh into the phone, like those brief hits of Northern California wind that come from nowhere out of the sunshine and push all your hair into your face, unsettling an otherwise pleasant day. The sigh made you sound like you had lived a long hard life even though you were twenty-eight years young and seemed to lose accountability like a sock in the wash.

So it's a best-sister speech then, I said.

I guess, you said, and before we hung up I reminded you that I hadn't put you on the spot at my wedding, and you reminded me that I hadn't asked.

YOU USED TO WRITE to me when we were young; I'd find messages tucked into my shoe or lunchbox. Back then all of your letters were a signature combination of great feeling and formality that I've come to miss very much.

To my sister: Your the best sister in the whole world. From, Danny Larsen.

Hello, I love you HEPPY BIRTHDAY Sincerely, Your Sibling

Even now, as adults, I still hear it in your voice mails. *It's me, Danny*, you always begin, as if I won't recognize the number, or the sound of your voice.

ONCE, WHEN YOU WERE A TEENAGER, I wrote you that angry letter—do you remember this? I was home from college and handed it to you on Christmas Day, for effect. You tossed it on your dresser where it remained unopened the rest of the week and, feeling remorseful by then, I took it back and tore it all up.

The letter was about money, of course, as most of our fights would come to be. You'd taken cash from our mother's underwear drawer a few days before and bought a silver bracelet for a blond girl at school. (How much I could say in the speech about your lifelong appreciation for blond, blue-eyed girls.) When our mother discovered the bracelet in your backpack, you'd pretended the gift was for her, the dangling hearts so clearly unintended for a mother. In reality you hadn't gotten anything for our parents for Christmas yet, and I'd just put both our names on whatever I had. When you asked me what the letter said as I packed my car to head back to school, I said it explained what I thought of you when you did things like that.

Your body settled into this statement and from across the driveway I watched the words warp into some strange shape for the journey ahead, through your ears, your frown, your throat, your heart.

Well, you said after a moment, what do you think of me? You said it so earnestly that we both couldn't help but smile. The question seemed absurd after so many years together, and I didn't end up answering before I hugged you goodbye.

———

YOU ASKED ME WHAT IT'S LIKE to be married, what we did at home if we had no TV.

Talk, I guess, I'd answered, and your eyes widened like it was the last line of a ghost story.

I'VE THOUGHT ABOUT US OFTEN over the past few years as I've tried to become a mother. I've thought about simpler times: like when our parents went out and we'd have pizza delivered and you'd squeeze the blue cheese dressing on our plates for dipping like I'd taught you. We'd watch whatever you'd picked out at Blockbuster because in about thirty minutes you'd fall asleep. Sometimes you'd fall asleep still holding the pizza, your little legs crossed on the couch; I was probably about fourteen, which would make you eight. Your head would slide back, your mouth open, and then when I'd take your plate your body would slide over to me, slumped dead-weight on my shoulder or lap. At this age our days no longer contained physical closeness; I no longer picked you up or swung you around or carried you on my shoulders as I once had. I was fourteen and bodies were becoming new territories to me, mostly my own, and I no longer touched people without awareness. But on nights like this I would let you take full comfort in sleep, I would cover you with a blanket and finish your pizza and occasionally if you stirred I'd rub your back. What surprises me after all these years is the fear I still feel in talking about your body, a body I've known and lived next to for so long, a body I've hugged and pushed and carried and cleaned.

Were there simpler times? Was anything ever simple for you?

I TELL MYSELF I CAN'T WORRY about the speech. I can't worry about the speech in a place where everyone will have drunk too much and you'll be so busy being famous for a day that you'll hardly remember the words at all. I tell myself that I'm a last-minute substitute, which should keep expectations moderate at best. I tell myself that the success of a marriage does not depend on the success of the speech, and if it did there would be many more luckless unions in this world.

Maybe I worry because I've watched our parents plan with your bride for the past six months, how money has again translated to care. Where have you been? Maybe I worry because I want to be good for the three of them, because I've refused to do anything just for your sake. I helped with the cake, the color scheme for the bride, the backstage drama of who would sit next to whom. I helped with the flowers and finding our father a tie, the silverware, the chicken or steak; I conceded to wear whatever the bride picked out. I tried to help with the absence of the bride's parents, and how our parents shouldered the costs as a result, but too often I became angry and ungenerous and consequently no help at all. I was angry most of all because of course I still loved you, because everything was always done for that reason, despite what I told myself.

When you called a month ago about the speech, I realized I had never put words to that kind of love, or more specifically *our* kind, and how it had always felt a little different from everyone else's. I didn't know how to angle it into the light, to see through it, and instead I longed to just buy the cake and wear the dress and show up on time to explain that I love you. Because what did I know about which facts should be collected or shed in the story of a person? What right did I have to speak of your life?

I F I WERE TO START from the beginning, I would say that you entered the world on May 28, 1991, ten minutes after eight in the evening. Your birth certificate, which now sits in the box of paperwork next to my bed, tells us you were born at home, with only a nurse present. The address listed is difficult to trace, but if you widen your search to Samut Prakan, suddenly your corner of the earth appears. For the first nine months of your life you lived there with your family just south of Bangkok, at the mouth of the Chao Phraya River on the Gulf of Thailand, on the western side of the province. You know this because our mother and father told you, but it's not something you asked about while growing up.

But I always wanted to know more about the baby I never got to meet, because hard facts were the most intimate records we had, and so from about eight or nine years old I memorized your paperwork the way children learn their favorite book. You were three thousand grams, roughly six pounds, six ounces, when you were born, and your name was Boon-Nam Prasongsanti. Your mother was named Nin and was thirty-two years old at the time of your birth. Your father, Chet, was thirty-six. Both of their identification numbers are listed on your birth certificate, though, coupled with their names, still return no search results. Years ago, when I first saw their names, I remember thinking that your mother seemed awfully old to be having a child. Thirty-two, I said to myself, probably horrified. Now it strikes me just how young your mother was, how quickly she had to say goodbye to you. I wonder if she knew from the beginning that there wouldn't be much time.

There was one other person present at the birth, a Mr. Kit Foythong, age fifty, who, according to the home address provided, appears to have been your neighbor. I don't know why his is the face I can imagine so clearly, the neighbor, whose role in the delivery may have been critical or merely passing, stopping by only afterward with a pen. His relationship to you is listed as *Other*, and it is his signature that certifies the report of your birth.

I don't know how long your mother labored, or what, if anything, she was given for the pain. I don't know if there were siblings also present at the birth, as the certificate lists you as *Child No. 4*, something that was initially withheld when we first came to meet you, and confirmed finally when our parents knew to ask, though no other information was provided about the three children before you. In fact, of the period between your birth in May 1991 and the July day in 1994 when we first locked eyes on you, we know very little. We know that your mother had nine months with you before she passed away of liver disease. Judging by your eyes and bright, straight teeth, your thick hair and walnut skin, I imagine she was very beautiful.

Of your father we also know very little. The paperwork from the orphanage documents him solely as *handicap*, and our parents were told he couldn't earn his living and depended on food from his temple. Shortly after your mother passed, he gave you to the Department of Public Welfare. He signed the forms that referred you to your first orphanage, Phayathai Babies' Home, on March 9, 1992, and it is at this point in your paperwork that you begin to be called an orphan. The orphanage told our parents that your father likely didn't have much longer to live, though at the time, with all the blank pages they'd been given about you, they weren't sure what to believe.

On December 2, 1992, you were transferred to the Rangsit Babies' Home, where you were considered legally available for adoption. Records indicate that you never had any serious illness in either orphanage, only the common cold, fever, and common diarrhea, though we wouldn't learn this was untrue until two years later, when we'd finally meet you.

OUR MOTHER KEPT A DIARY during the first three years of my life, where every sound, outfit, sleep pattern, expression, and clip of dialogue is recorded into three small drugstore notebooks. Sometimes the entries are on scraps of paper stapled in, written quickly with a free hand or during a few quiet minutes while I napped. I've often wondered why you never seemed curious about the early years of your life, but then I'm reminded that I wasn't curious about my own—I'd never asked to see the diaries until recently. When I was certain I didn't want children, the diaries were of no interest to me, and then later when I realized I did, they were too difficult to think about. But lately I've found myself turning to them.

We have no pictures of you as an infant, no diary, so I'm left to imagine how handsome you must have been from the beginning, with your toothless smile and signature frown. I imagine that your mother took you right away in her arms and began to forget all the hours of long, painful work. I imagine your father sitting at the foot of the bed, and Mr. Kit Foythong at the door with the nurse, offering congratulations. I don't imagine you cried much, because tears have been rare in all the years I've known you, even when you're scared. Instead I imagine you pressed yourself against your mother's chest and breathed a sigh of relief that your hard work was done, too. I've never imagined this scene with other children in the room, even though there were likely three siblings nearby while your mother rocked you, maybe sang you a song.

Have you ever wondered whether you were held, tucked in; if someone was keeping track of your sounds, your sleep, your happiness?

I WAS SURPRISED to see our mother mention adoption in those diaries from my first few years. The seeds of a life's path are so often scattered by the thoughtlessness of the wind, but there it was: the bud of a future with you. Maybe it's just surprising to read about any kind of longing from a parent. Though I remind myself that the woman in the pages is my age.

In one entry, when I'm seven months old, she describes the new visions that batter her head: I'm choking on a button or blinding myself with a toothpick or acrobatically flipping out of the crib. The rare times I sleep through the night she shakes me awake to ensure I'm still breathing. Our father, in the background, is bewildered. As I read, I wondered if anxieties like these could be understood without children. I remembered that when I first fell in love with your brother-in-law, I would put my hand on his chest while he slept or watch him walk away down the street and think please, please, please. Please never die or else.

I wonder what adoptive parents feel, she writes. *Is it the same? Is there a physical bond because she came from me? I've wanted to adopt a child and wonder if there's a difference. I've acquired a lot more love for her since the day she was born so maybe it's the same, after all. Maybe I would love as I learned to know.*

———

RECENTLY I CALLED OUR MOTHER and asked her again about when she knew she wanted to adopt, and why, and she said what she always said, that it was just something she always wanted to do. As a teenager, on cold winter afternoons, she would take the bus out to Sea Cliff after school and spend the last hours of daylight at St. Christopher's, an orphanage in Long Island, with a building full of children, from toddlers to teens. It was a bright attempt at a home, as she remembers it, however temporary, with windows that overlooked the bay and a staff of adults who soon became her closest friends in Long Island. They stationed her in the library, where she taught children from five to nine years old how to read and write. When I asked her if there were any children she became especially attached to she said yes, that there had been one in particular, a little boy. She said the memory of him had stayed with her for many years, though she didn't offer much more on the subject.

MAYBE YOU JUST DIDN'T WANT TO be pregnant again, I said a few days later on the phone.

Oh, please, our mother said, in the way she has our whole life. You know the voice I mean. *What am I going to do with the two of you.* She reminded me that adoption was something she had always thought about, even dreamed about, the way some women dream about conceiving.

YOU REMEMBER HOW I was in my teens and twenties: I took pride in saying I didn't want marriage or kids. We lived in a place where children grew up and stayed, multiplying to keep the Catholic school running, and I longed to escape a cycle. It never required much of a leap, that certainty that a disinterest in marriage and children made me not only different but better, like the sexy aunt in the movies who comes to shake up the family on a weekend visit. That kind of woman always seemed to have lacy underwear, a bottle in her purse, a wrecked beauty that, back then, I found enviable.

What I never told you was the shock that came in my thirties, the kind people talk about but I'd never believed to be true, when I started to imagine my body with a baby inside it. Suddenly my brain was host for biological takeover, and the invasion spread to your brother-in-law, too. Almost overnight he began clucking at children on the street, on social media wearing funny hats, while I dreamed of the powdery scent of a baby's skin, the softness of their feet, the heat produced from pressing them against my chest. I dreamed of an imaginary child with the wistfulness attached to romantic longing. It was a desire without a history, like new skin grafted to a body, a foreign organ implanted. But the old resistance was still in there, too. I pictured myself swollen, constipated, the acne returned to my face, leaving it cratered like the moon, its blemishes visible a planet away. I pictured rock-bottom fatigue, the carpet a plastic minefield, a pillow over my face to capture the scream. I had heard what the disruption would kill off temporarily—sleep, sex, two minutes alone in the bathroom—but no one could confess to the larger question: What were the permanent losses?

In truth, I knew what disruption felt like in a house, how it stayed with you even after you left. I remembered how the world transformed with you, and I wasn't sure if the two fears belonged to each other. I wasn't sure if this had been the root of the resistance all along. It began to eclipse so much of my thoughts that finally one morning I went to the doctor in secret, suddenly starved for the cold, objective truth of a medical professional.

I told her I was scared about what a baby would do to my body, my life. I told her lately all I dreamed of was babies, and in the dreams I was happy, but when I woke I found myself steeped in sweat. And instead of telling me it was all right, that I was a normal person, which I realized halfway through was the reason I'd paid to come, she told me I should prepare to be patient, for women like me who have follicles on their ovaries the process could be arduous. Arduous, she repeated, after my question. She reminded me there were always other options. Would I consider other options?

YOU AND I HAD DINNER the day of that appointment. This was four years ago, and you must have been living in Reno. You were visiting our parents in Petaluma and had driven into San Francisco to see me. I asked where you wanted to go and you said California Pizza Kitchen, and I said we could go someplace nicer but you said you liked their barbecue chicken pizza, that there was a shortage of good barbecue chicken pizza where you lived.

We were getting along well in those days; there was no wedding yet, no talk of you returning to Thailand. You were working hard to get your degree but as usual all you wanted to discuss was girls. You usually preferred your brother-in-law's advice but since he couldn't make it that night you were stuck with mine. I listened until finally you said, What's your problem, anyway?

Problem?

I drove over an hour to get here and I can't tell if you're pissed to see me.

I'm not pissed to see you.

Are you mad that we came to California Pizza Kitchen?

This made me laugh, and then your face softened but only a bit. I sat back in our booth and for a moment I considered it: I'd told you when relationships had ended, when I'd been laid off, when I was worried about your brother-in-law or our parents, but somehow I couldn't bring myself to tell you the truth. Somehow I couldn't just say, plainly and without much consequence: Danny,

I think I want to be a mother and today someone told me it might not be possible.

Instead I said: I'm glad you came. I'm just stressed about work, no big deal.

Why? you said, and you meant it.

Boring stuff, I said, and waved over the waitress for another beer for me and a Coke for you. I asked you to tell me again about the girl you were seeing now, and you pulled out your phone to show me a picture.

OUR MOTHER AND FATHER began researching the adoption process in 1989, as you've been told many times, when I was four years old. Adopting domestically was out of the question; it could cost upward of thirty thousand dollars and they couldn't afford it. So for roughly two years our parents searched; they were both over forty years old at this point and many countries were closed to them because of it. They looked in Central and South America, but in many instances the adoptive family was required to stay in the child's home country for weeks before they had clearance to leave with their new baby. You were also expected to grease some palms down there, according to our father. China hadn't opened up yet; South Korea had shut down its adoption process after Bryant Gumbel called it a baby factory during the 1988 Olympics. One afternoon our father received a phone call from his old college roommate and the advice was brief: consider Thailand. I hear you can have a child in six months.

But then: three more years of waiting. Our father was laid off, sending the three of us from the East Coast to Petaluma, California, where we lived with our aunt for close to a year. I remember swimming in the outdoor pool of the neighborhood complex at Christmas and thinking how wonderful this was. I didn't realize that more bad news had come: California law required our parents to do most of the adoption paperwork and in-person screenings all over again. They were transferred to another adoption agency, which, once we moved out of our aunt's house and into the small rental on the west side, began the process of sizing us up.

First thing, a social worker began visiting us at the house. We welcomed Rosemary Pascal into our living room wearing our finest—our mother and I in long floral-print dresses, our father in his one sweater-vest—and introduced ourselves with trembling hands. I hadn't known to feel nervous until the doorbell rang and I watched all the color leave our mother's face. Our father went to answer the door, and unsure of what to do, our mother and I followed. We all stood there a little strangely for a moment, smiling at the visitor on our doorstep, until our father remembered to invite her in. Our parents had done these screenings before, but maybe the prospect of rejection seemed scarier now because they were even older, with fewer alternatives. Our mother had put out cookies but I was the only one who ate them while Rosemary asked me about school and hobbies, questions I returned with ease. It wasn't until she asked if I wanted to be a sister that I looked at our parents, afraid that there was something wrong in the question. Of course, I remember saying, a little irritated. I don't know if my mom and dad have told you, but we've already waited so long.

Rosemary took some notes and it occurred to me that maybe the baby wouldn't come because of what I'd said. How was I supposed to know the stakes for this meeting were so high? Why had nobody told me? I held back tears on the couch while our mother remained pallid and our father navigated Rosemary's questions about his recent unemployment, crossing and uncrossing his feet.

Danny, if you could have only seen us. We must have looked like the unhappiest family in the world. There was so much I didn't know about our parents' money problems, work concerns, but they never wanted you in order to fill a hole. When our father would come home from his new job, our mother and I would run to the door to greet him, singing *yay yay yay*. This is what I knew. We had a good life. We wanted you to be a part of the happy thing we had going, despite the money, the moves, the jobs, the waiting.

SHORTLY AFTER THAT DINNER at California Pizza Kitchen, I started going to a fertility clinic in San Francisco, not far from my office, passing long mornings in the waiting room. Despite high infertility rates among nonwhite groups, and less research on the issues affecting those demographics, the waiting room reflected another truth: it was white, upper-class women who had access to medical interventions or, as in my case, women with health care that actually considered reproductive health.

A fuller portrait of longing was often found in the forums online. There definitions of womanhood weren't limited to having a working womb or having a womb at all. Women pooled recommendations for Black OBs; others asked about doctors who were LGBTQ friendly. There no one called IVF a tool of the patriarchy; often we wondered where the feminists were when it came to us. Instead we could try to put words to the force field that surrounded mothers, whereas we were unsexed, sites of a hollow desire, of an unnatural, scientific labor rather than a God-given one. I participated in these conversations and I didn't; they weren't a utopian escape. People fought in the forums, they corrected and insulted one another, they contested milder forms of sadness, and problems presented often remained unsolved. But talk was open and there was compassion: we wept and hoped for those we'd never meet, those who vanished once success found them. It was just that the waiting room was lonelier. In person we avoided each other's eyes.

I used to think that a fertility clinic would be the kind of place where women cried while they waited on the couches for their names to be called. But most of us waited for our names just as we wait for the bus. Once a man came in with his girlfriend and looked at us waiting-room women as if we were contagious, as if he were going to start his period on the way home. This may be the reason I always preferred to come alone. I liked the feeling that we were all banded together against something while we waited, even in our silence.

To make someone wait: the constant prerogative of all power, Barthes writes.

Sometimes while we'd wait I'd hear the nurses' laughter in the background and think, why not share the joke? I felt like telling them: those of us out here can appreciate a joke as much as anyone. But then I remembered that there are people in this world who want you to be a little bit apart, as you know. They want to know, I suppose, that they're safe from the things about you that scare them.

WHILE I WAITED, sometimes I thought of you. I thought about how secrets change. When your brother-in-law and I first started trying for a child, it felt like the most exotic secret we'd ever made together, second only to falling in love, and we carried it around for weeks, holding it as close as a child itself.

When the weeks of trying turned into months, the secret suddenly felt too heavy to keep; I told our parents and one or two close friends. I didn't have the strength to air it out to everybody, though seeing it written here that doesn't appear entirely true. I don't know why I held it so close for so long, if it was shame over my body or maybe just over my desire, that yearning for a typecast role was reductive. I began to wonder again, as I once had, if my life would be better without children. Why else would my body turn against me. Why else had it become a broken thing?

I WASN'T SUPPOSED TO DRINK once the treatments began, which ruled out the bars. And I'd lost interest in walking downtown after work, galleries and bookstores replaced by new businesses, all named after sounds that a baby might make. *Kaggle. Zynga. Digg. Hadoop.* So I started going to the library a few times a week in the evenings, walking up Market Street to San Francisco's main branch.

Sometimes I would hear you as I sat there reading, reminding me of the night you turned twenty-one. Here was your sister, late to the family dinner again because she couldn't decide on a gift, and ended up at the bookstore, circling for an hour. She finally decided on *The Catcher in the Rye* because it was one of the first books our father had given her, and she remembered how significant it'd felt at the time, some rite of passage that signaled she was ready for a world with drinking and prostitutes, so different from the one that she knew. She hadn't known that books or the world could look like that, or sound like that. Catholic school had not provided that narrative.

When she presented the gift to you back at the house you looked at the wrapping and frowned. Really? you said, without even opening it, the hurt genuine. Do you know me at all?

MY HUSBAND AND I were young when we met in graduate school, filled with a kind of romantic impatience, waiting for life to get on its way. It made all the days drag and sparkle. We went for a drink after class and when he asked how old I was I answered, Almost twenty-five. Almost twenty-five when, he said, and I winced and told him. That's nine months from now, he said, smiling. Yes, I said, gulping my drink.

Sometimes when I picked up books from young writers at the library, I'd want to tear all the pages, chew them, and spit them out. Get a job! I would tell the characters. Money and blood never seemed to concern them, how they'd eat, where they came from. Maybe the more time passed, the more fictional old selves became. Maybe they revealed the same person years later. Or maybe I'm still re-covering from the idea that I won't become any of the characters I'd once hoped, having grown into a career at one of the city's tech companies instead, the kind I used to complain about. That first job was meant to be temporary, but that was many years ago now.

How do I still not get what you do? you'd said.

The more important you are the harder it gets to explain your work.

You're not that important, you said. Come on. In five words or less.

So I explained it to you, first in five words, then in ten.

Huh, you said.

Does that actually help?

Yeah, you said. But it makes me a little sad for you.

IN THE BEGINNING I traveled for work because I enjoyed it, and later because it was easier for me than for my boss; without children I could quickly pick up and go. When I would call you at airports or while waiting for a cab—all the pockets of time one fell into while traveling—you would ask if my life was getting fancy and I would correct with the reality of the scene. *I ate alone every night. I for-got to pack underwear again. The flight was delayed and the thing that I came for didn't go through.* Like Dad, you would say, the comparison always surprising me. And we'd remember together how he would come home after a week away and we'd swarm him with the small details of our days, unconcerned with where he'd been, what had happened to him.

EVEN WHEN YOU GREW into a man's body, I always carried that inch or two over you; I always had to look down to consider you. I also had those nine long years before you turned up, which I'm still not sure you've forgiven me for.

Nine years was a long time to be an only child, though, and perhaps not something to be envied. Childhood didn't pass as quickly without the slick surface of chaos; being an only child was mostly a waiting game. There was time to settle into oneself, to become accustomed to the quiet, to learn to talk to myself under my breath. *Solitude, great inner loneliness,* Rilke writes. *Going into oneself and not meeting anyone for hours . . . Loneliness of the kind one knew as a child.* I don't recall being lonely. Only lately have I thought about who I became in all those free hours of childhood, building up a quiet little island from books, population one, a place where you could never reach me. Our mother began reading to me early on and language became the bridge between us. If I was hit with a rumble of anger or need or hurt or confusion, I was instructed by our mother to explain why that was. I never considered the enormous advantage in all these things until you came, when I was left to imagine an entirely different kind of silence, so different from the one I knew. To be three years old and have no words or expressions to draw from, minimal Thai, no English. I don't need to explain to you how deeply the first few years of our life affect the outcome, tracing the ghostly shape of who we're destined to be or who we'll hardly escape.

I had spent those early years in a home you would never know, a small one-story far from California's dry climate, with a pond in the backyard and green carpet in my bedroom, a house that, shortly after we left it, was demolished and replaced with something much larger. But back then, the heat rose up from the floors and in winter I associated the mornings with bare feet on the embers of the kitchen tile. In the summer, fireflies would blink in the backyard and the house would fill with the scent of cut grass. And in the front our father planted our first Christmas tree, whose bottom branches we decorated every December.

It was there in that little home where I grew alongside the anticipation of you, imagining a sibling at four, five, six. In the beginning I could hardly wait, asking our parents again and again when a sibling would come, until eventually expectancy became so common that I no longer felt compelled to ask. But I never feared or dreaded your arrival, and this is truth, because in my naivety I didn't think it would change anything. I pictured our life with you as an extension of what already existed. Back then it felt like the three of us against the world in the long fight to get to you.

So we were bound by that little house, we were bound by wait and process, and of course we were bound by the body, too. Adrienne Rich describes the connection between mother and daughter as a knowledge that is subliminal, subversive, preverbal: the knowledge flowing between two alike bodies. This knowledge lived in the comfort I took in our mother's body: her lap, her neck, her hair, her hands, her voice, the ears that announced themselves when she pulled up her hair. It was an ownership I felt, in the way a child would show an adult her room, with the confidence that each object inside it was hers to touch, to test, to name, to hold close to her chest while she slept. This knowledge extended to our father, too, because in his body I found proof of myself: there, marked up all over him, were my fingernails, the curls that wound around the base of my neck, sense of humor, legs, that miraculous alchemy of nature and nurture that continued to bloom. A parent could spend a whole life in fear or admiration, depending on the work nature had done.

SOMETIMES IN THE WAITING ROOM I'd think about which secrets became acceptable to keep. I still hadn't told you about the treatments, and I'd think about how or why that had happened, as if it were a decision separate from me. For a while I told myself it was because I was the older sibling and didn't need to burden you. But there was the other part, too, all this work being done to modify my body, all the shots and pills and routine ultrasounds, structures put in place to prevent or prolong what might be the next question.

Hypocrite, I would imagine you saying, reminding me of the health scare our father once kept from us. I often thought about that in the waiting room. How we were both moved out and grown, both furious. How after a final positive report from the doctors and a few glasses of wine, he announced the good news to us one evening over dinner. No special occasion had brought us together—you were driving through town on your way to see a girl, and your brother-in-law and I had joined at the last minute to see you. Maybe it was the spontaneity of our meeting that made the news that much stranger, or perhaps it would have felt strange either way. Six months? I said, ignoring his relief. You lied for that long? You looked at our father and said nothing.

You tell this story differently. You say that I was the one who sat there quietly. That you were the one to call him out on his mistake.

What difference does it make?

Because I was the strong one, you said, while you just sat there in the corner feeling sorry for yourself.

Sorry for myself? Why?

Because you don't like thinking about death.

Oh really, I said. I was laughing now.

I don't know, you said. Your voice became quieter and I couldn't tell where your mind had gone.

I don't know, you said again, I just try not to ever think about it. And then I was quiet, too. I didn't know if you felt like you knew something I didn't. It was true that the thought of him gone had invited a terrible loneliness to the table, even as we all sat around it. Maybe my childlessness had also bound me to our parents; my only concept of family was a nostalgic one.

Some days I don't know what frightens me more, the idea of life without children, or without parents, or being the only parent you have left.

ON JANUARY 25, 1994, at 7:30 a.m., after five years of waiting, the adoption agency called our house. This is the call, the woman said to our mother on the phone, we have your match. I leaned into the receiver and together we listened to your name: Boon-Nam Prasongsanti, born May 28, 1991. Later, when I saw your name on paper, I realized how beautiful it was, the first part like a drumbeat, the second like a few melancholic notes on a stringed instrument. But I didn't hear this at first when she pronounced *nam* like *ham*, *santi* like *panties. Boon nam praw song santi.*

Our mother put a hand to her mouth and then looked at me. I remember her initial look of happiness and relief, and how quickly those feelings were transmitted. Then she dropped to the floor, apologizing to the phone while she sat on her knees. The tears frightened me because I didn't understand them; I didn't understand all the longing and sadness that was shackled to the joy of that moment. After she hung up we walked around the house together, each space suddenly renovated with the news. This was the room where you would sleep, no longer an office; this was the room where you would eat, no longer just a table for three; this was the room where you would play with me, no longer a child without the company of a sibling.

Our father was away that week on business so our mother dialed his hotel in New York, but he was out. She decided to leave a message with the receptionist, whose voice was cool until our mother said, Tell him he's a father again!

Oh! the receptionist cried, suddenly all sweetness. We could hear motherhood warming her voice. What is it?

It's a baby boy, our mother said.

OFTEN PEOPLE HAVE ASKED how we prepared for your coming. For four and a half years our parents didn't know the sex of the child; for a portion of that time they thought they would be adopting an infant. Eventually they found that, the younger the child, the longer the line, and that biological parents were legally allowed to reclaim them up until their first birthday. So our mother told the agency that we would be thrilled with whomever we were matched with, and put away visions of carrying you through the door. Instead we imagined whoever you were to us then, walking through it yourself.

HOW DOES ANYONE PREPARE for a child, I wonder now, regardless of the route you take. I knew one family from church who had been through the process—I babysat their two kids, adopted from Mexico. But even that situation seemed different from ours, as both children looked like their adoptive parents. Our father says they read lots of books, that our mother marked up each paper from the agency with scrupulous underlines, even when she was unsure exactly who she was underlining for. The image of you was blurry for so long, after all; we didn't receive your name, age, or picture until a few months before we met you.

I have a memory of asking our parents at dinner if you might be bullied for looking different—but I'm not sure this is right, whether this came up before or after the bullying had already begun.

Did we assume that any hurt you felt would only come from outside the home and not from the trauma of living within it?

THE FIRST DOCUMENTED transracial adoption in the United States was in 1948, between a Black child and a white family in Minnesota. Up until that point, and even still afterward, Black families were denied adoption services, making it difficult both for Black children to find placements and to find placement within Black homes. Transracial adoptions grew in the postwar boom with rising interest from white families, but some states continued to ban them through the fifties and sixties, even after laws barring interracial marriage were ruled unconstitutional. In the seventies, the National Association of Black Social Workers changed the course of the conversation when it issued a statement on transracial adoption, which took a "vehement stand against the placement of Black children in white homes for any reason." It argued that white homes weren't equipped to raise a Black child in a racist society, that these adoptions were done for the benefit of the white family rather than the welfare of the child, and that Black families would adopt in higher numbers if the adoption process didn't effectively eliminate their applications. The statement echoed throughout the community and Black–white placements began to decline.

There were fewer public discussions around transnational adoption at this time, how a child from an Asian country, for example, might psychologically adjust to a white home, white still being the primary demographic for American adoptive parents due to money, access, and racial bias. This was evidently an easier narrative for the culture to swallow; a kind of institutional saviorism was less apparent when foreign children came into the mix, not as quick to remind America of its original sin. But there was little mainstream language for any of it yet.

There was a connection between the two things, though. It was true that our parents couldn't afford to adopt domestically, but controversy might have stopped them if they'd traveled farther down that path. At its peak in 1970, only an estimated 2,500 adoptions between Black and white families were finalized each year, and the more controversial the subject became, the more international adoptions began to soar. They accelerated throughout the seventies, eighties, and nineties, when Americans would adopt more than a quarter of a million foreign children, most coming from Asia, Eastern Europe, and Latin America.

I say all of this to you now because, in the privacy of our own home, the three of us didn't talk about it before you got there, because our parents, in spite of the tall piles of research, perhaps didn't notice the space a blind spot can occupy. I picture us there at the dinner table and am surprised to see how easily we slotted into adoptive tropes, either in the unspoken hope that we could make your life better, or that we ourselves would be changed, altered, transformed in some way, converted from a white status quo.

And yet. Here also sat the same family, so excited to meet you. Here they sat, turning over your papers like love letters from afar, longing and praying for the wait to end. Any concerns our parents confided in each other might have been brushed aside with two questions: Here in this progressive California town? With all the love in the world to give?

———

MY HUSBAND AND I had a game for a while, Bad Empathy, and the contestants comprised both friends and strangers. To qualify they needed to say things like:

Is it him or you?
Just relax!
You have plenty of time.
It could always be worse, like cancer.

Ding, ding, we'd say to each other in the beginning, when we still had a fresh sense of humor. This week's winner. Step over here to the side to receive one giant foot to stick in your . . .

One evening at the library I picked up *Who's Afraid of Virginia Woolf?* I'd forgotten about the younger couple, Nick and Honey, who have married because of Honey's hysterical pregnancy, a condition more palatably known in the medical world as pseudo-cyesis, in which nonpregnant women believe they are pregnant. What's most mystifying about the condition is that their bodies convince them: their breasts and abdomens get larger; they experience nausea, vomiting, food cravings, and missed periods; in some cases they come back with positive pregnancy tests due to hormonal shifts that can only be half explained. Hippocrates documented this as far back as 300 BCE; Mary Tudor and Freud's patient Anna O. were said to have experienced it. I was reading theories around its connection to desire until I saw a text from my husband, asking if I was ever planning on coming home for dinner.

On the train, I went back to the play. I'd remembered how George and Martha's sadness violently propelled the drama forward, its true horror kept secret until the final act. And I'd remembered the reveal: a child invented to bind their private pain closer, for better or for worse, an apparition part angel, part demon, that after twenty-one years would finally vanish that night. And so I didn't think I'd feel chilled by the play's conclusion until I came to one of Martha's final lines just before the lights dim, as George invites her upstairs to bed.

Just . . . us? she says, and it feels like the loneliest question in the world.

DAYS AFTER THE PHONE CALL, your picture arrived in the mail; you know the one, the famous first picture. Our mother debated whether to wait to open it until our father got home from New York, but our aunt was over and said, What—are you crazy? Open that envelope. So our mother secretly peeked in at you, before running upstairs to show me, and I said you were the cutest baby I'd ever seen. In that first photo, you're two years old and standing on a stretch of concrete with a brown awning overhead. To the left is balding grass, and the sky is bleached from the bad angle. You're standing to the side, head cocked toward us, like an inmate who's misheard the instructions for his mug shot. You frown. You're barefoot, with white shorts that display prancing red-nosed reindeer, and they're pulled up over the bulge of your belly. Your shirt is yellow and green and says CASPER THE FRIENDLY GHOST! with a smiling, sickly-looking ghoul on the front. From this side angle, one thin arm is visible. Despite the frown, you are such a handsome toddler that the look of unhappiness almost suits you. Your eyes are large and brown; your cheeks puff out, only to narrow into a dignified little chin. Your small lips curve downward. You offer us a look at one small ear and a buzzed head.

That day, I removed one of the photos from a frame in the living room, slipped yours inside, and asked if I could keep the picture in my room, where it sat for many years until the day I moved out, and took it with me.

It still sits in the same frame on my desk, just far away enough from the window to protect it from the sun, one of a handful of photos from those first three years of your life.

SOON AFTER YOUR PICTURE CAME, the adoption agency recommended we make you a Life Book. So our mother bought a thick blue journal and taped a copy of that first photo inside, a copy of your birth certificate, our packing lists for Thailand, and other to-dos before meeting you. Later she would staple in pages from the journal she kept during our trip to meet you, cards from your first Californian birthday, your baptism, an outstanding participation award from school. It rested on a shelf in your room where you would always be able to find it growing up and remained there after you moved out.

Looking in your box of paperwork recently, I found the outline for the Life Book provided by the adoption agency. *A LIFE BOOK can help you deal with the mundane issues that uniquely built families will encounter*, it explained. It included a template to get started, in case any new parents got stuck:

> *Not so long ago, on [date] a little [boy/girl] was born in a faraway country: [Korea/India/Thailand]. [His/her] name was _____ and this baby was you. The woman who gave birth to you knew that she could not take care of you because [she was not married/she was very poor/she was very sick] and knew that she couldn't give a child all the things [he/she] needed.*
>
> *We don't know what the woman who gave birth to you in [Korea/India/Thailand] looked like, but because you are so [handsome/cute], we imagine that she must have been very beautiful. What do you think she looked like?*
>
> *Before you came to us, you were taken care of by a [foster family/ayah/orphanage] in [Korea/India/Thailand]. You lived there for the first [months/years] of your life. Then on [date] we got the call that it was*

time to meet you. Imagine our excitement! [Insert story of first meeting, joy at finally holding child. Include pictures.]

You didn't sleep well for the first couple of [days/weeks/months] because you were probably kind of scared. We looked and smelled very different from your [Korean/Indian/Thai] [foster family/ayah/orphanage]. But gradually you relaxed and accepted us and knew that we were your forever Mommy and Daddy [plus siblings, if applicable]. Soon you felt very much at home with your new family. [Pictures.]

Now you may look somewhat like the woman who gave birth to you in [Korea/India/Thailand], we don't know for sure, but we do know that you [walk just like Mommy, tell jokes like Daddy, etc.]. Because we love you so much, we think about the woman who gave birth to you and your birth father and hope that they know deep in their hearts that you are safe and happy and deeply loved. No matter which way parents and children become a family, they all love each other, and they will be a part of the same family forever.

I was struck by this strange little guide; I was struck by our mother's decision to keep it. It reminded me of those Hallmark cards with text that filled both sides of the pages. *I know I wasn't always easy growing up, but you've always been there, Mom . . .* I often wondered about the people who purchased them, if they signed their names at the bottom with relief, off the hook for anything other than an endorsement. I looked back at the Life Book instructions again. Was this the narrative we also had followed?

IN FEBRUARY, our parents mailed the papers that said they would accept you and purchased a white teddy bear with long, soft fur to include in our package to be forwarded on to you. At the last minute our mother had the idea of including a key chain around its neck with our photos so that you might recognize us when we came. Our mother started to slide in a group shot of the three of us, but then felt strongly that you should be included, too, when you looked at it. So she and I pulled out the albums and searched for three single photos of each of us, then slid them in alongside one of the few small, single photos we had of you. We all kind of stood on top of each other inside the frame but I agreed it was better; I tried to imagine you studying us.

For a long time our parents had discussed giving you an American name that closely resembled the Thai, but they couldn't find one that worked. They decided on Daniel, the biblical interpreter of dreams, because it was a name from our mother's side of the family. Our father said he would call you Dan, but I knew even then that would never stick. You would be Danny. Danny Prasongsanti Larsen.

In April, a date was set to meet you: July 4, 1994. It was coincidental that you would join your new American family on the most American day of the year, and our parents' friends marveled at the timing, bound up in the symbolism of some American dream. Our parents nodded politely, just grateful a date was confirmed, grateful for any information, really, that continued to come in, little by little, to help assemble some picture in their minds of the boy who would be living with us. These papers would usually offer one more photo of you, followed by a set of facts: height, weight, immunization records. Sometimes they'd include a short summary at the end that did nothing to help us imagine you: *In general, he is a healthy child, his development is suitable. He is quiet but not afraid of the strangers. He can walk and run stably and can climb up the stairs.*

BEFORE YOU, our father used to quiz me on the state capitals at dinner. I'd ask him to do it. What a ridiculous little portrait of an American family, our meat and starch, our plastic place mats, the child rattling off Juneau, Bismarck, Little Rock, Lansing. On Saturday afternoons our father liked to watch TV and on Sundays we would take bike rides. Back then I could never spot a joke coming on our father's face, not once. Suddenly his delivery would break through some firm inner membrane in which seriousness had been holding him captive. And then his body would release—the head thrown back, the teeth revealed—and the real punch line would be his own amusement.

HE CAUGHT ME once with a boy. Something you probably never wanted to know. I was seventeen and taking the pill every morning, terrified about what would happen if I swallowed it five minutes late. That afternoon he came home early from work, and when he walked through the door all the curtains were open, exposing my room to an ugly, bleached sunlight. I sat up in bed and the boy hid his face under the covers.

He didn't yell, as you would have guessed. He looked at me and I looked at him and he said nothing before turning around, the door clicking shut. He said nothing later that night at dinner, or the next day, or the next. I didn't go out for weeks after that, as if to put a punishment on display.

How did you know how to make him laugh? I wish you had taught me that gift, how to soften trouble. Like when you knocked out the light on his car and went straight to McDonald's before coming home, delivering a Happy Meal with the news.

Why on earth, he said, as you handed it to him.

I just thought it would make you feel better, you said, and before he could tell you how ridiculous that was, his head was already thrown back in his chair.

HERE'S SOMETHING we did to prepare, our mother said recently. She slid a paper across the kitchen table. It had the words *mother, father, older sister, hungry, pee,* and their transliterations in Thai. One day in the months before our departure, suddenly frantic that she wouldn't be able to speak to you, she'd driven to a Thai restaurant on the east side of town and asked the woman behind the hostess stand if anyone there spoke Thai. The woman raised an eyebrow, and when she learned the reason, that a soon-to-be mother wanted to speak to her son, she said no. What could she have thought about this white woman who would be raising a Thai boy in her home? What could she have told her that wouldn't take a lifetime?

When our mother turned up again the next day the woman sighed, sat down in an empty booth in the back, and conceded by scribbling down some phrases while our mother ordered what she hoped was an expensive dish.

Can you imagine it now, our mother driving across town once a week to practice her pronunciation off the back of a paper menu, where new words and phrases were written in pencil? Our mother would try to keep them in her mouth the whole drive home, where she would later repeat them to me and I would recite them at the dinner table, the state capitals now replaced. *Mae, paw, pee-sao, hiu, shishi.* Later that year they brought you back to the restaurant to introduce you to the woman. Do you remember this? The woman knelt down and spoke softly in Thai and you hid behind our mother's back.

Just speak English, the orphanage had said when we got there.

AS OUR DEPARTURE NEARED, our mother cooked her way through the Thai recipe book she'd found at a garage sale. I have no memory of what she learned, only that she tried, and that the staples in our home were none of those things after you came. What we loved:

Hershey's Syrup, Chef Boyardee, Bagel Bites with the little pepperonis. Kraft Mac and Cheese and Froot Loops.

Our father bought me a textbook called *SIAM*, not meant for children but probably all he could find with plenty of pictures. I don't know what happened to it. But I can still see the spires of Wat Arun that seemed hardly contained by the page, stock photos of elephants and monsoons. I held them against the backdrop of our tract home, the squat shops of downtown, the summers that made you forget about rain, and wondered how we would make you feel happy. I had no idea what your life looked like so I tucked it within the book's beautiful things. Red flowers and god-swept clouds. I hung a picture of an elephant in your room and your new sheets were patterned with baseballs.

THE LAST HAPPY MEMORY I have of those months was the surprise baby shower our aunt threw for our mother. We walked into the house one Saturday afternoon in May to a roomful of smiling faces and a banner that read: WELCOME, DANNY! (24 LBS—OUCH!) There was cake and clothing to be unwrapped and a tangible excitement in the room. About a week later, though, the dread set in: our parents were still missing one signature on the last of the INS paperwork. They needed FBI fingerprint clearance—without it, the U.S. Embassy in Thailand wouldn't allow them to take you home and our mother, in the final days of her final trimester, started smoking again.

With three weeks to go, our father found the number for the FBI and began asking every person he could find for help. The adoption agency had gone silent, and there were no replies to his daily messages. Our father faxed our files to Congresswoman Woolsey and Senator Feinstein, and their offices replied that they would call Immigration for us.

This is the part of the story you've heard many times, but I wonder if you've ever been able to see how much fear was built into those final days, a desperation that we might not get to you. Our departure date was June 27, 1994. On June 23, there was still no word on the fingerprint clearance and our father called the senator's office again. After five years of preparing for this day, he found himself suddenly at the mercy of one administrative staff member at Immigration. Was it actually possible? he kept saying, pacing the house. To come this close and be stopped by one person's mistake?

On June 24, our mother woke at 6:30 a.m. to find that our father had been up since five calling the FBI. He went to work and our mother brought me to Mass so that she could pray the rosary and beg. When we returned home we distracted ourselves with our packing lists, acting as though the scene was normal, as though there was nothing potentially stopping us from packing at all. I kept moving for our mother, knowing only that to stop any momentum toward you would be the very worst thing. I worked for most of the morning compiling a bag of toys and games for your long plane ride home. We were packing the last of your clothing that afternoon when our father called.

Sometimes, as an adult, when you're frustrated with one of us or feeling left out, you get this look that seems to say, *Are you even happy I was born?* It's another one of those expressions singular to you, hard to pin down on paper, and when I try to describe it, strange images pile in: storm clouds suppressing rain, a buck planted in the middle of the road, weeping Madonnas trapped in stained glass. I see it when I cancel plans, when our parents say no. It's a look that asks if you are wanted, and to those who understand it, it's punishing.

In times like this, I wish you would picture our father calling the FBI and telling them he was with Senator Feinstein's office. He gave them the name of one of her employees to prove it, though I still have no idea how he obtained it. By process of elimination, beginning with the switchboard's general number, he was eventually referred to a woman who handled fingerprint clearance. He gave her the employee's name, told her our story—that we were scheduled to leave for Thailand in three days and were still missing the signature required on our final fingerprint clearance to bring our child home. She said he should call Lydia Finn at INS.

At 9:00 a.m. he was outside the INS office in San Francisco. The lines were long already, over two hundred deep. He stood in the same spot for close to three hours before another idea came to him, and he made his way over to the private offices. He began knocking on doors, one by one, telling each person who answered that he was late for his appointment with Lydia Finn—where might she be? Thankfully, miraculously, he finally found her office, though it took a white man skipping the line at Immigration, and I wonder now how, with another family, another's life, the circumstances might have shaped up differently. When he walked in, she looked up from her desk and said, You! You're the one who has every senator and congressperson in the state calling me!

She said she'd call her contact at the FBI in D.C., but she made our father leave the room. When she let him back in he couldn't tell whether the news was good or bad, but she said she could get the clearance in writing via mail. Impossible, our father said, we're leaving Monday. So they faxed it.

Our father told our mother this on the phone, and then went back to work. She wanted to send balloons and flowers to his office signed from you but when the florist asked the occasion, she began to cry. I took the phone, gave the credit card number, repeated the message for the card. With a nine-year-old's sense of great purpose I made the additional calls, one by one, to our parents' friends, delivering the good news.

WITH OUR FATHER, love was understood in acts of service. He filled our cars with gas, brought home the ice cream we liked. He repainted your room when you decided, after two weekends of labor, that you'd changed your mind on the color, after all.

So when, a few years ago, our father spent an afternoon in the garage and pulled out his letters from Vietnam, I wondered if this, too, was in service of love, since we'd always been curious about this part of his life. He'd mailed the letters to New Jersey fifty years before, addressed to his parents, and his mother had saved every one. They were stuck in a green file folder marked NAM and one day he gave them to me, just like that.

I held the letters and asked if he'd waited until this particular point in my life to show them to me, on the cusp of starting my own family. To which he answered: Actually I just kind of forgot about them.

So I took the letters home, and our father said no rush, and as soon as I walked in I started reading. Eventually your brother-in-law turned off the bedside light and I took the folder onto the couch and sat there until I'd read every one.

And what does our twenty-two-year-old father sound like? The year was 1967. He arrived in Da Nang on a 120-degree day in July, and the letters continue until Thanksgiving of the same year, when an explosion sent him into the air and then into the hospital. He describes the eighty men put under his care, the heat, the food, the mosquitoes, the children from the villages who came by to sell Popsicles to the platoon. His handwriting is the same, and a joke here and there, but that's about it. He is a young, handsome stranger on paper, with a calm that can perhaps be attributed to being twenty-two. The omission of the violence backstage only seemed to make it more ominous, and I was embarrassed to realize that in reading I felt the same as I'd felt in life: disappointed because the stories had been stripped of the details. His greatest concern is keeping his men safe, a group of men who are younger than our twenty-two-year-old father. In the back of the folder is a sandwich bag that holds his Purple Heart, and a note from a woman in Potlatch, Idaho, thanking our father for letting her know how her fiancé died, what a relief it had been that he went honorably and without pain. As I read I couldn't let go of the feeling that I was somehow still missing half of the stack. Though what had I really expected to find? I read and reread them for days afterward, then weeks, as if by extracting, turning over, and polishing each story, it would reveal some deeper message. *Have to go, to the rescue*—he signs off.

Maybe they also made me wonder about the narratives we inherit, about what does or doesn't get passed on. Without a child of my own, I didn't know what would happen to my stories, my letters, my sentimental items and junk. Would you want any of it? I offered our father's letters to you once if you remember, and you said, Do they talk about the war, and I said, Kind of, and then you never asked about them again.

If you had read them, you might see a trace of the same man who, thirty years later, would call the senator's office, who would wait in countless lines and fight the ones in which he couldn't afford to wait. Or perhaps I can only read with the knowledge of the man and the father he would become.

I returned to them again in search of you, in thinking about the speech. I asked our father if Vietnam informed his desire to adopt, but he only frowned, as if to say that those kinds of connections only happened in the movies. He reminded me that adoption had been our mother's idea.

ONCE, DURING A BAD SPELL with you, I told both of them I would never adopt. The point then was not whether I meant it, but that I meant its desired effect. The hurt on our mother's face. I can still see it now, many years and apologies later.

ON JUNE 27, 1994, we packed the last of our things, returned borrowed books and videos, mailed letters, picked up traveler's checks, and made copies of all the papers our father had worked so hard to get. Panic started to set in that we wouldn't get everything done, but we walked out the door on time at 5:00 p.m., as our mother took one last lap around the house, to ensure your first glimpse of home was a clean one. We arrived at SFO, comforted ourselves with bowls of clam chowder, and then completed the first, brief leg of our journey, a one-hour flight to LAX. There, we were told our flight to Hong Kong was delayed by an hour, and the three of us fell asleep in the stiff black seats at the gate. Our mother woke up at some point to our father reading the paper, telling her we must wait some more. She went back to sleep. We left U.S. soil at 2:45 a.m.

WE ARRIVED IN HONG KONG in the early hours of June 29, 1994, where we had a three-day layover. If our father hadn't worked in travel, I don't know how we would have afforded that trip. It was two weeks on the other side of the world, an otherwise mammoth expense without his discounts on flights and hotels, and costs that couldn't be reduced were put on a credit card to worry about later. We went straight to a Holiday Inn and spent most of Wednesday asleep. Our father wondered aloud on the car ride to the hotel if and how the Babies' Home had prepared you to meet us, and in our heads a kaleidoscope of scenarios played: tears, refusal to leave with us, remoteness. I'm sure I was afraid then, head pressed to the window. I'm sure I had never felt so far from home.

The next day, to distract ourselves, we went to the Temple

Street market. I remember mostly the heat that pasted our clothing to our bodies, turning the curls on the back of our father's neck
wet, a heat so different from the dry summer days I'd never thought
to notice at home. I remember the crowds, and how our mother dug
her nails into my wrist so that they wouldn't swallow me up. I'd never
seen so many people in my life, and felt dazed by the white noise of
language around me. I thought to ask our mother for something
cold to drink but since I couldn't read any of the signs I said nothing. At some point our mother tried to check in with me, to see how
I was feeling about the looming change, but I had spoken enough
about preparing to meet you over the last five years and now I just
wanted to meet you. Our father enjoyed the market immensely.

When we arrived back at the hotel I fell asleep, while our father
and mother sipped two cold beers on the bed. Eventually they
drifted off, too, but by midnight our mother was awake again. At
2:00 a.m. she got out of bed in a cold sweat, hearing only the sound
of her heart. I can't really imagine just how frightened she must
have been, alone in the middle of the night at the Holiday Inn, days
away from becoming a mother again, with no one to tell her how
it might turn out, this time so different from the first. Just a few
weeks before she had heard a story about a couple who had gone
to Romania to adopt their daughter and then, upon witnessing the
child's emotional detachment as a result of neglect in the orphanage, decided to go home without her. She'd brushed it aside when
she'd heard it at home in her kitchen, but now the story rattled
inside her like a shot of caffeine. She went into the bathroom and
closed the door. On the toilet she recited Psalm 91. *You will not fear
the terror of the night, or the arrow that flies by day, or the pestilence that
stalks in darkness, or the destruction that wastes at noonday . . .*

ON JULY 1, our father and mother awoke at the same time, around 4:00 a.m. They were married ten years that day. Across the pillow they whispered to each other until the light traced the curtains, though neither of them remembers what they talked about, or if they do, they've chosen to keep it between them.

We walked to the shopping district in the afternoon, exploring a large complex by the Star Ferry. Our mother said that she had never seen so many expensive clothing stores in her life; our big purchase was three Mrs. Fields cookies. We took photos of the harbor and tried to find a nice restaurant for the anniversary dinner. On the way back to the hotel our mother bought two pocket-size hand mirrors with jade handles for thirteen American dollars because she thought they would make a nice gift, though she knew no one at home expected souvenirs from this particular trip.

Our last evening in Hong Kong, we ended up at an Italian restaurant for dinner. I pushed my minestrone to the side mid-meal, laid down my head, and gave our parents some privacy by falling asleep on the table.

THE NEXT MORNING we boarded an early flight to Bangkok. We checked into the InterContinental Hotel, set down our things in adjoining rooms, and then walked to the Siam Center, where the most bustling attraction was the Pizza Hut. To prepare us for our arrival, the adoption agency had sent an abbreviated list of logistical and emotional pointers: *Only 220 volts for your hair dryer. You may find yourself overwhelmed by the anticipation of finally meeting your child. Dress up for the embassy, NO JEANS. Don't be surprised when you are out in public with your Thai child that you will be constantly stared at—it's okay! By all means, sample the Thai cuisine; it is an unforgettable experience.*

ON SUNDAY our father went to the hotel pool while our mother and I took a cab to the city's Holy Redeemer Church, which displayed a large gold statue of Christ with arms raised to heaven, as if to say, *Well, here we are.* Our mother was nervous about getting back to the hotel without the internal compass of her husband, but we found a *tuk-tuk* for fifty baht, a ride that made us both smile girlishly for the first time since leaving home.

Later, we pushed through the crowds of the Tokyu Department Store in search of last-minute gifts for the social workers. But this day, more than any other, was marked by feelings rather than by comings and goings or new sights and sounds. There was sadness along with excitement and fear, because change is always tethered to some kind of departure, some send-off to a life you knew.

At dinner I said that this would be the last meal with just the three of us. We were as ready for you as we'd ever been—at nine, forty-five, and forty-nine—and yet; what a strange course in preparing for a child, we must have all thought then, in communion and in isolation. We raised our glasses and toasted.

WHEN A WOMAN'S BODY FAILS to conceive on its own for one year, the first thing they do is run a genetic screening for 176 conditions, taking enough blood to fill a kiddie pool. They test for things with names like 11-beta-hydroxylase-deficient congenital adrenal hyperplasia, CLN6-related neuronal ceroid lipofuscinosis, Herlitz junctional epidermolysis bullosa LAMB3-related, and something called maple syrup urine disease. Blood is also taken for the thyroid, for the follicle-stimulating hormone, for estradiol, for the anti-Mullerian hormone; there are routine checks for varicella, rubella, HTLV, HIV, hepatitis B and C, clearance forms for Zika. There are new Pap smears to put on file, mammograms, and a procedure called a hysterosalpingogram, which x-rays the uterus and fallopian tubes in search of abnormalities.

Hysterosalpingogram. I kept thinking about the word while on the x-ray table as some kind of exercise in practicing calm, trying to forget the origins of the word itself. *Hystera, hysteria, hysterical,* traced back not just to the Greek word for uterus but to a long history of gaslighting women. A doctor came in and repeated what I'd read in the paperwork: a catheter would be inserted between my legs, then a balloon would be inflated inside my uterus to hold the catheter in place, then the catheter would inject dye into my fallopian tubes, then the x-ray machine would begin its photo shoot, capturing any blockages in the tubes that would prevent the dye from passing through.

Any allergies to iodine? the doctor asked, and I said this was my first time dyeing my tubes so it was hard to be sure. This might feel uncomfortable, he said, and then a shot of air filled the balloon like a bullet. When I cried out his face reappeared over my legs, more out of curiosity it seemed than concern. Can I keep going? he asked, and I wondered if he was thinking I'd be no match for childbirth. Keep going, I said, and clenched my fists while the dye went in and the nurses stared up at the screen. Slowly my tubes lit while the machine hummed, like a neon light flickering open or closed for business.

Later in the doctor's office your brother-in-law and I stared at the tubes on the big screen.

Should they point that way? I was asking.

Depends on the woman, a nurse said, her smile friendly. There's nothing wrong with the way yours point.

Sitting there, I was relieved that the report had come back positive, but I still didn't trust the look of them, healthy or not. They look like a Demogorgon, I said.

No, no, the nurse said, shaking her head.

I looked at your brother-in-law for allegiance. They look like those dancing balloons in front of car dealerships, he offered, and I exhaled and reached for his hand.

TURNS OUT, most people have their own ideas about what makes a body primed for conception. Our aunt proffers cod-liver oil, nettle leaf, dandelion, and red clover; my neighbor overhears me on the phone with our aunt and gives me a book of fertility meditations, incense, and an unlabeled topical cream. A coworker comes over and suggests removing all the gluten from my apartment, which deeply saddens your brother-in-law. A friend, slightly more with the times, recommends sex with my legs straight up and downloads an app that supposedly chimes when I ovulate, signaling that your brother-in-law and I must rush to the bed.

In the beginning I actually found a kind of relief in the fertility clinic, in the solidity of procedure. *Somebody professional has a plan.* I couldn't pronounce most of my drugs but following their instructions provided a path forward. The doctor prescribed medroxyprogesterone, clomiphene citrate, and choriogonadotropin injections and in time the science project of my body became less and less strange. Medroxyprogesterone for ten days to induce the periods I'd stopped getting since I went off the pill. Five days of clomiphene citrate to stimulate ovulation. Then, if a follicle grew large enough, the timed choriogonadotropin injection at home on the couch. At 10:00 p.m. I'd lift my shirt and your brother-in-law would rub disinfectant below my waistband. The first time I told him I'd do the injection myself because I'd seen the way he tried to kill spiders, how many lives had been spared in our apartment over the years. But when I pulled the needle out from the package it was much larger than I'd expected and, after seeing my face, he took it from my hands, instructing me to close my eyes. I heard his finger tapping the air out of the needle and then the soft voice he reserved for moments when I was scared. Then the puncture and his free hand on my back. *Almost there.* It was such an odd moment between us that I find myself thinking of it often, some new form of sex. I didn't know then that these requests for help would soon become like cutting a tag or unsticking a zipper, that in time I would just do them on my own. After six months passed, I asked the doctor if there was anything else that might help my chances. Any special vitamins, unlabeled topical creams? He said I was doing the thing that was helping my chances. He told me to spend a few afternoons a week at the gym on top of the other activity.

SO I STARTED going to the gym on my lunch break. I did this, I told myself, to fend off the expectation, because I'd begun to wonder if I couldn't tell what was beautiful anymore, that I was losing track of which thoughts were mine and which were the world's crowding into my head. Sometimes I swam laps in the pool, but most of the time I just ran. It was a lousy gym if you looked closely; there was an ant problem in the showers and lockers, the machines were often broken, and if you forgot a rubber band for your hair you had to pay a dollar for some old one from the drawer. There were stains on the white towels. But again I felt comforted by a routine. Motivational commands were graffitied all around me on the walls, saying things like PERSPIRE TO SUCCESS and ENERGY IS CONTAGIOUS and GOALS ARE MADE TO BE CRUSHED.

There was the man at the front desk folding towels who told everyone who walked in, Welcome back! as if they'd been missed the last six months.

There was the woman who always forgot where the towels were and walked around fretfully, approaching people at their machines, yelling over their headphones, Where are the towels? Please, where can I find the towels? And someone would stop, catch their breath, and show her the way.

But the locker room often surprised me. How many different bodies I saw, how many types of people. Here was this space just feet from the ordinary world and suddenly women were baring breasts and baring feelings and walking around with no makeup or apologies; those few feet at the entrance were where all the rules changed. There were the showboats who stood in front of the mirror naked, bending over to blow dry the backside of their head; there were the corner-dwellers who turned away while they changed, as if punished, choreographing an impressive routine with their towel. There were tattoos and birthmarks and burn marks; there were long purple scars and small bedpost notches; there were barbelled nipples and hair, hair, hair. There were those who came in and out without a word, and those who talked loudly with their girlfriends while they dressed, passing stories of illness, of men, of money, of bodies. I heard a lot of talk of the body. I felt like telling them, your energy is contagious. I felt like telling them they looked great. Sometimes while I was in there, corner-dwelling, I wondered if I would have been a showboat if I'd had a sister, if I'd grown up in a house with another small body reminiscent of my own.

There was one woman I hoped to see each week, and did, usually on Tuesdays and Fridays. Her back was curved into an uppercase C. She did weights with a trainer, and sometimes she swam, and she was eighty-nine years old, I heard her tell her trainer once. She took the highest locker on the wall to avoid bending, and pulled the bench over to stand on when retrieving her clothing. She was a showboat, too, standing on that bench as naked as one can get, like she was about to make a motivational speech. Sometimes I wanted to ask if I could help her, but I feared saying anything to take away the shamelessness of her body. So instead I just offered a smile, the one woman in the locker room I allowed myself to make eye contact with.

These were the types of things I told only our mother. Sometimes I'd wonder: Could I tell you stories like this when she was gone?

IT WAS AROUND THIS TIME that you came to see me again in San Francisco, and I'd decided to come clean to you about the fertility treatments. The secrecy was starting to feel strange. You'd driven in to see me on my lunch break, feigned surprise when I paid for your pricey sandwich. You looked like college had just ejected you into the restaurant via Nerf gun: sandals, surfer tee, sunglasses sunken into your thick head of hair like two frog eyes peeking out from a dark, black pond. You'd graduated and received your first job in Web design in Reno. You were in the mood to boast.

I let you boast for a bit. I was happy to see you; the frequency of your calls had decreased dramatically over the past year but I think it was because you were happy—you'd just started dating your future bride. I'd stopped asking about your arguments with our parents, scripts I usually knew well before I heard from you, though you were always selective in which fights you brought up.

By the end of the meal I was surprised to find myself nervous; I'd never been nervous with you in my life, except for at the very beginning and, even then, I was probably too young to stay nervous for long. Now, staring at a grown version of you, I noticed my voice speeding up; I looked away from your eyes for a moment. So, I said, readying what felt like a confession. The restaurant by my office was too noisy, filled with the restlessness of a nine-to-five lunch crowd, and I paused for a moment as a large party settled into the table next to us.

Then you said: Did Mom tell you about my trip?

Trip?

I applied to a mission trip, you said.

Where?

Twelve months, twelve countries. Thailand is month two.

What about your job? Your girlfriend?

She's okay with it. The job will help me save.

What will you do?

Charity stuff. I'll send you the website.

You never told me you were thinking of going to Thailand.

I'd be going to lots of places.

Do you think you'll be accepted?

I don't know. I hope so.

The waitress came and refilled our water and then suddenly it was you who couldn't look me in the eye.

ONCE, ON AN AFTERNOON spent in internet wormholes, your brother-in-law and I googled the name of the town where you were born. We discovered that numbered villages divided it, and that your village was number 14, just south of the inlet of water that came in from the Chao Phraya River. We went down the wormhole some more and found that the numerical system for home addresses was based on the order in which they were registered with the county office, so plot 81 could sit next to plot 43, and we quickly became lost again; it felt impossible to find answers in the map's gray area. We wondered if the area had been swept over by some natural disaster or remained completely rural or had been taken over by the military complex that was now marked on the right side of the province. There didn't appear to be many roads, either; we did find a Tumblr account that seemed to prove this theory, which offered images of small boats that carried people along what looked like a lengthy bank of mangroves.

Your brother-in-law was the one who had figured out that the transliterations were inconsistent on some of your paperwork. This hadn't occurred to me; I'd taken all of your documents as gospel, likely because when there were so few facts to go on, the ones presented inevitably felt more solid. But your brother-in-law was accustomed to handling unfamiliar words on a page; he found a thrill in searching, rearranging, until clearer answers came into focus.

Ah, he'd said. That's better. Here. And we'd leaned in to examine the town called Laem Fa Pha, translated by Google as Cape Lightning. There was a phone number listed for the district office and I dialed across the world before hanging up after the first ring. Why should I expect they'd speak English? And what would I say?

It felt like I'd walked into a private conversation of yours, and I didn't tell you or do it again. But I wondered how different this was from the way I'd once memorized your paperwork, or the frequency with which I'd lately revisited it. Where was the line if you were my brother? It hadn't seemed to bother you in the past but maybe at some point this had changed. I hadn't asked.

Everyone always thinks I don't want to talk about Thailand, you always said. *But I just don't remember anything so I don't have anything to say. How can I talk about it when there's nothing to say?*

I DON'T KNOW WHAT TO SAY, I said. This was the first time in your life that you'd expressed an interest in returning to the place you were born, to the orphanage where we met. I didn't realize that I'd always pictured us going back together, that I'd believed the return should be done just like the beginning. I didn't realize that the return seemed to promise some change in the distance, a passage from one era to the next, toward some brighter beacon of enlightenment, where we all might feel a hint of its warmth on our faces.

I'll take lots of pictures, you said, maybe sensing that I was upset, and my whole body filled with shame. I was ashamed of the secret I'd kept from you, a secret whose weight I hadn't even admitted to myself. I was ashamed of my assumption that you'd need me in order to go back, to be guided toward some redemptive meaning. Or that you would guide me.

We hugged each other goodbye on the street and it wasn't until after you walked away that I finally faced a desire that, until that point, had been unknown to me: I had wanted to inscribe myself in the memory of those early years, where your other siblings would have been.

WE WOULD ALL COME to remember the day a little differently. What can be agreed upon is that we woke early on the morning of July 4, 1994, none of us having slept, and dressed quickly and silently. The drive to Rangsit was one hour from our hotel, and the man at the front desk translated our directions to the orphanage into Thai on a piece of InterContinental stationery. We walked out to the front, where another hotel employee hailed us a cab, and our father handed over the directions to the driver.

Nothing was said in the cab, not even when we finally saw the sign for the Rangsit Babies' Home an hour later, turning into the long dirt driveway. I stepped out in front of a gray concrete building and watched the driver ride away.

We were directed to an air-conditioned waiting room to meet Khun Preeda, the social worker. She told us that if you didn't scream when we met you, then it would be no problem to take you today. Our parents looked at each other blankly before following her to the wing where the babies slept. You were napping and they needed to wake you to inform you that your family was here, so we waited outside on a small blue bench. Our father remembers he was too nervous to sit, so he stood while I held our mother's hand.

Finally, a child wandered to the door. Years later I can still see his face, bent into a scowl, as if threatening to beat me up in the parking lot. And I was suddenly deathly afraid, staring out at the features that I would be called to love.

This is not him, Khun Preeda said, to my relief, and it wasn't until a few minutes later that another boy wandered into the doorframe, accompanied by a caregiver. This is him, Khun Preeda said, and in your hand you clutched the little white bear. Though I would have known you from anywhere.

Then the narrative splits, as I recall sizing you up before kneeling to hug you. You frowned at me, but I was grateful to find no malice in it. *I can't say I know what's happening*, the frown seemed to say. *I woke up from my nap and now this*. And I knew, kneeling there, that I would be able to love you, and feeling your little body in my arms, I was already getting the process started.

Our parents, meanwhile, knelt down to hug you and saw a large head battered with white powder, then cocked their own to examine it. Immediately they spotted the malnutrition: your head wobbled on your shoulders, your stomach was pregnant with illness, and two thin clubs held you up—your excuse for legs—with black knobs for knees. You looked at them in a stupor, and they looked at each other and thought the same thing: Is there something they haven't told us? Khun Preeda saw their faces and said, He is just tired, still sleepy from his nap. Our parents were unconvinced.

Then she said, I have something I must tell you. Our parents braced themselves. She'd been concerned about your weight loss in the last few months and wanted to take you to the hospital. She said they had two choices: they could leave you at the orphanage today and pick you up at the hospital tomorrow, or they could take you now and meet a social worker tomorrow at the hospital.

The offer to leave you was tempting. The three of us looked at one another and considered delaying the responsibility—a beautiful night of postponement took shape in our minds. We would return to the hotel and go straight to sleep, forget all of this. We would sleep to escape the dreamlike state of the afternoon. Our mother looked down at me and thought, This, after five years of waiting, and now the offer to wait some more appeals. Despite my best efforts to love you immediately, even I imagined an evening free of you and looked back at our parents, grateful that I would not be making the decision.

Don't be hurt by this. I hope now, years away from that day, you see the humor above all else. Here you were, this frail little thing, and the three of us were scared to death of you.

Our mother spoke first, looking at our father. No, she said. I think we should take him today, let's get started.

All right, he said.

Before signing the last of the paperwork, our parents asked to see where you slept. Khun Preeda led us to the door, where we slipped off our shoes and climbed two flights of stairs. The interior was gray, bare, and smelled of urine. We stepped into a room that slept fifty, bed touching bed, children sprawled out in all stages of rest. Those still awake looked up at me, while one older child shut his eyes and turned his head. You didn't cry or make a sound as we inspected your room.

I kept my eye on the older child. This would be the detail that stuck, as the rest of the room would pass away into the state of forgotten things. To see so many babies and toddlers here had less of an effect; it wouldn't be until much later that I would process what I'd seen, what a different picture of the world this day had provided, thousands of miles from the white suburb where I lived with our parents, modestly but comfortably, attended Catholic school. But at the sight of this older boy peeking out at us—he must have been seven or eight years old. He looked so overgrown in that bed, turned away from us, a giant bookmarked in the row of all those babies, a puzzle from the magazines in the dentist's office that asked, *What's wrong with this picture?* A mismatch I could usually spot before my name was called, running my finger over some three-eyed fish or nightstand without any legs, just floating there in the middle of the frame. And a new kind of loneliness filled me, as our mother reached for your hand and we turned to walk away, to leave the grown boy and the room full of children behind. Five minutes earlier I might have asked our parents, *What will become of him?* because I was a child who had grown up in the company of adults and thought I preferred honest answers. But in the middle of your room, I wondered about honest answers; here the truth seemed only complicated. I'd had no idea that your life looked like this; our parents hadn't prepared me, maybe because they were unprepared themselves. I turned away and followed Khun Preeda down the stairs, collected my shoes, took your hand from our mother's, and led you to the office to finish the last of the papers.

Back in the waiting room, our father pulled out the clothing we'd brought for you; he'd been told by the adoption agency that it was polite to ask if they'd like us to leave what you were wearing. They said yes, so our father began to change you while our mother took note of the holes in your shorts. Our mother continued to fill out the forms when suddenly you laughed—what a sound!—and the whole room stopped to look. Our father had tickled you while changing your shirt and you let out a giggle, so foreign from the expression you had given us in your photos, and over the course of the last hour. Our parents felt their hearts lighten. Our father gave you some crackers from the table while Khun Preeda answered our mother's questions about your eating habits, sleep routine, history. She asked if there was any information on your first tooth, first step, first word. Khun Preeda shook her head. Our mother asked again about siblings and Khun Preeda answered no, then looked to you; you were busy devouring the snacks on her desk. You should take care to stop him when he eats, for there are only clean plates in the orphanage, she said. Soon you were on your third cookie.

At this point it occurred to her that a copy of your schedule might be useful. She pulled a piece of paper from her desk, with writing in a combination of English and Thai, and slid it over to our mother. The English said:

6.00—Get up, toileting
7.00—Breakfast
9.30—Snack
11.00—Lunch
11.30—Toileting, bath, take a nap
2.00—Snack
4.30—Dinner
5.30—Toileting, bath
6.00—Playtime, watch television
7.00—Prayers, bedtime

Then: the last of the signatures, thank-yous, pictures. I handed the social workers the gifts that had been suggested by the agency: soaps, boxes of cookies. A cab was called and, dressed in your new blue outfit with matching Barney hat, you stepped into the back seat, on our mother's lap. I climbed in and examined you, trying to gauge signs of distress or remorse at leaving the third and most long-standing home you had known in your life. I discovered before Khun Preeda shut the door that this was only your second car ride. You held your little white bear and were the only one who did not raise a hand to wave goodbye to Khun Preeda as we pulled away, back down the dirt road.

I feel like I'm dreaming, our mother said.

You fell asleep almost instantly. None of us can actually recall how far we made it peacefully—likely thirty minutes, our father now says—before our mother looked down to see a small stream of fluid dripping from your mouth. This is the part of the story you loved growing up, one of the few details you asked about again and again. And what happened when she reached for the tissue? you'd say. She reached for a tissue but before she could get to it you began to heave; a white, warm vomit sprayed all down the front of your outfit and on our mother's skirt. The driver's eyes found our mother's in the rearview mirror and, from the front seat, he handed us a plastic bag and roll of toilet paper without the cardboard tube in it. You heaved again. Now you and our mother were covered before she could get the plastic bag under your mouth.

I screamed, a rancid smell filled the back seat, and the driver sighed and pulled over. Before we could get out, you'd started up again and our father held out his hands in front of your mouth, cupping them. You filled them with more liquid, a clearer consistency this time. You paused and we took the opportunity to leap out of the car: our father shook out the contents of his hands on the grass; our mother placed you on the ground and began to strip you back down; the driver popped the trunk and found an extra roll of paper towel while I batted off some of the spray that had landed on me.

We piled back into the car; there was another emergency stop made before we reached the hotel. The staff at the curb greeted us kindly and helped with your soiled clothing. We were too frazzled to wonder what we must have looked like, all piling out of the car, outfits soaked, new child half naked, as if we'd just come off some terrible ride at a water park. You didn't cry but you realized something was wrong; your face had gone sullen again.

We brought you to our room and hoped you didn't think it was home. Our mother turned on the bath and only then, when you'd been stuck in the tub, did you begin crying. It was an ugly sound, a wheezy, kazoo-pitched cry, and it scared me. Our mother noticed again how thin you were: twenty-four pounds at three years old. She took your picture, and when the flash went off you cried harder. She made a note to bring the photo to the doctor when we returned home.

Our mother scrubbed you down. If you were going to cry anyway, she figured she might as well give you a good clean. She rubbed the bar along your skin, avoiding your genitals. She rubbed your dirty nails and shampooed your scalp and shielded the rinse from your eyes, and when the water turned off so did your tears. She wrapped the white hotel towel around you, rubbed your back cautiously. She wondered what your buzzed head would look like when your hair grew in. Again you frowned at her. *Might you tell me where I am?* the look seemed to inquire. She wished she could speak to you, but now every Thai word she'd memorized back at home fled from her memory. She dressed you in another pair of clean clothes that was also too large. Then she brought you into the room where I sat with our father, waiting quietly.

I took out a toy truck we had brought and sat across from you on the floor. I rolled it toward you. You looked at it a moment and then stared at me with watery eyes. I pointed to it. I took the truck back and rolled it to you again.

You pushed the truck, and it rolled to a stop halfway between us. Good! I cried. Our applause was met with another frown. I'd had a hard time envisioning what playing with you would be like, but I might have hoped then that in time you'd do a little better than this.

Our father, meanwhile, sat at the little table next to where you were rolling the truck. He was noticing something, had been noticing it since we arrived at the orphanage this morning. You would not look at him. He had asked Khun Preeda about the male caretakers at the orphanage, and she said all the caretakers were women. In the chair, he tried to come to terms with the truth. You were afraid of him. After all they'd been through to get here, how much farther would he have to travel to reach you?

At dinner that night in the hotel restaurant we ordered you a Caesar salad and plate of pasta. You chewed quickly and silently and finished everything. While watching you eat, we began to eat ravenously, too, bottomlessly. We pulled from one another's plates except yours. We gulped our drinks, ignored our napkins. We licked our lips for traces of comfort. None of us had heard you speak.

By the time the check came, I was tired in a way I hadn't known about before. Back in the room, I went into the bathroom with our mother to get ready for bed, and, when left alone in the room with our father, you began to cry. He knelt on the floor and held his arms out to you, but you shrieked and backed away, an eruption that made the earlier tears seem amateur. Were they really beginning like this? our father thought. I had never looked at him with the dread that you did then. He took the truck and rolled it toward you as I had done, but you stared at it and wept some more. He moved toward you, which you answered with another kazoo cry, warning him not to come any closer. Our father wondered if he might cry, too, before I came in and scooped you up in my arms, and the tears died down.

At nine o'clock, our mother brought you into the adjoining bedroom and laid you down on the twin bed. She tucked you in, and your eyes stared wide. Would you sleep through the night? I waited to hear you cry when she left the room, but you didn't make a sound.

Here you were, taken from the women who cared for you, your playmates, your bed. You were already three years on this earth and any people that could speak to those years had once again vanished. What were you thinking as you lay there alone? The room was cool and silent. Our mother left the door open a crack and went back to the family she knew, with the child who had lived with her for years, inside her for months, who she'd known as part of her before she'd met her. She kissed me and said I could stay in our parents' room as long as I liked. I was a little nervous; I'd never shared a room with a sibling before and didn't know what you'd be like in the night, if you'd cry, or make strange sounds, or watch me in my sleep. I decided to give you a half hour before I went in. Our father stared at the TV on low volume, and our mother lay next to him and put a hand on his stomach.

Then we took a long sip of quiet as the shock settled to the bottom of our stomachs. We drank in not having to speak to one another; we drank in mindless, familial ease. We refilled our cups with silence and drank some more. It wasn't until our father turned off the TV that we heard the noise from the other room.

We looked at one other, afraid to move.

What is that? I mouthed. I tiptoed over to the door, our parents following behind. We pressed our ears to the opening.

Our mother was the only one who felt relief at the noise. I pressed my body close to our mother and rather than listen to you, I listened to our mother breathe. And our father's heart broke in a way that felt both familiar and completely new to him. It broke at the sound of his son singing, a boy who could croon himself to sleep in the dark but could not bear to be alone in a bright room with his father. He listened to you sing, a soprano sound, a self-lullaby, the words unknown to us all. Our father was, in his own way, the most sentimental of all of us, and would return to this memory years later, he told me, on a morning when he missed you.

THE NEXT MORNING our mother took us to meet another social worker, Khun Sunan, while our father headed to the embassy. Following Khun Preeda's instructions, we took a cab to the Children's

Hospital, a place that reminded our mother of Grand Central. Through the maze of children and parents and signs we couldn't read, our mother finally spotted Khun Sunan by the area for blood work. When your name was called, we stepped into a small room and sat you on a chair. I braced myself for tears as the nurse pricked your finger, but all you did was furrow your brow. She took quite a bit of blood, I noticed, but you just continued to frown, looking up at me once, though I had no idea what to say to comfort you. I wanted to promise that our regular life would be much more fun than this, though I was impressed by how tough you were. This would follow you throughout your life—the one, comet-tailed tear when you fell off your bike and broke your thumb, the whimper I heard when you cut your forehead in the tub and needed stitches. Then the nurse pressed cotton on your wound and told you something in Thai. You lifted your other small hand and held the cotton there.

Once outside, Khun Sunan told us it was time for the urine sample. I expected to make our way to another room for some privacy, but Khun Sunan grabbed a cup from the counter and led us to a corner of the main room. She knelt and said *shishi* and pointed to the cup, and then instructed our mother to help you. I looked around us, embarrassed; I was still getting used to having your body around. I looked away politely while our mother pulled down your shorts but in a second my eyes were back again, as you began obediently peeing in the cup, and peeing, and peeing, and peeing, until it began to spill over the top. Khun Sunan and our mother cried out similar pleas in both languages—*Wait! Stop!*—while our mother ran for another cup, but by then it had hit the floor and was still going. When she came back with the second cup, you filled that up, too. Khun Sunan wiped up the mess while I giggled. I thought I caught a hint of a smile as you looked up at me.

We waited over an hour in the corner while tiny fans circulated the hot air. I remember nothing of the other families around us, only how disorienting the crowds were. Band-Aids and stained cotton balls collected in the corners of the floor and I might have noted this to our mother if Khun Sunan weren't standing there, too. Finally, the nurse came back and we followed her to the next area to have your temperature and weight taken, and then to the doctor, who sat in an air-conditioned space behind a curtain with five other patients. We sat next to a boy of eleven or twelve, accompanied by his father, who was being examined. When it was our turn, the doctor let out a small laugh when he realized our mother didn't speak Thai. Khun Sunan interpreted as our mother mentioned your chest congestion and how thin you were. The doctor laid you on a small table and again you submitted to probing, examining, a cold stethoscope pressed to your chest and back. The doctor said something to Khun Sunan and together they laughed. She looked at us and translated: He is so naughty, he says. We didn't tell them that aside from the singing the night before, we still hadn't heard you speak. We didn't tell them that a protest would have been welcome, so we might finally know the sound of your voice.

The doctor didn't say much about the cut filled with pus on your elbow or the unnatural curve of your potbelly or your cough. Instead he wrote out three prescriptions but concluded that in general, your health was good. So we headed to the hospital pharmacy, vacillating between skepticism and relief. After the long lines, more waiting in the limp, wet heat of the room, it was our turn and we received what the doctor had prescribed: an antibiotic, cough medicine, and vitamins. Then Khun Sunan hailed us a cab back to the hotel.

Our father, meanwhile, had spent the day on a chase for additional papers for the U.S. Embassy. We met him back in the hotel room and only our mother noticed how frazzled his face appeared. As he recounted the day, I sat with you and colored. You paused every few minutes to hand me a crayon, looking at me as if to let me know it was a gift.

THE NEXT MORNING we were scheduled to stand before the Adoption Board. Our father retrieved coffee for our mother while she dressed you in your best outfit from the suitcase.

We arrived late but found eighteen other white families in line waiting for approval; we were number seven. How strange the scene must have looked, the conveyor belt of white families in the middle of Thailand, circling in and out, the factory feeling of an experience that seemed, to all of us, so singular. Khun Sunan arrived and brought us to a waiting room with one large table, a basket of fruit, and a tissue box with a price tag from 7-Eleven. You kept yourself busy with your toy car, crayons, and a coloring book, and were quiet until you saw another family eating fruit. Then, for the first time, you pointed. Our mother peeled you an orange, which you ate quickly, before noticing a glass of pale soda. You pointed again and our mother let you drink. You pointed to an apple and ate the fruit along with its stem and core before our mother could stop you.

Finally, it was our turn, and we were directed into a U-shaped room, with the four of us at the curve. There were microphones for us to respond to the sixteen people who sat before us on the Adoption Board. One woman did most of the talking, asking if you'd cried and if you'd eaten, the second question seeming very peculiar since we'd had you for forty-eight hours by now. Another woman asked me if I was happy with my new brother. Yes, I whispered. And how will you help your mother? the woman asked, and I looked with fear at our mother. She's a big help already, our mother said. She added that I took great care to dress you and play with you.

All right, the first woman said. Everything seems fine.

We took that to mean we were approved.

AT THE BRITISH DISPENSARY for your official physical the next day, the doctor reviewed your pus-filled cuts, weight, and congestion with disinterest and signed the papers quickly. Afterward, our father picked you up and you started squealing and crying.

You began to smile, though, with a few days' history behind us. You followed our mother around the hotel room like the rattling tin cans on the back of a wedding car. Anything you could get your small hands on you'd pass on to her, as if weighted with the constant, self-inflicted pressure of having something to show for yourself. Each time food was placed in front of you, you'd look to her. If she said, It's okay, then you'd smile, eat.

It was incredible, actually, how quickly you were changing, right there in front of us. Your head seemed to sit more securely on your shoulders, you explored the hotel room with great fervor. You examined empty drawers, opened and closed the minibar fridge, turned lights on and off until our pupils hurt. You began to insist on pouring your cough medicine yourself. You peeled oranges, bananas, threw them back like peanuts. You found the on/off button for the television, the volume for the channels.

We did our best to keep up with you. While you groped for your independence, we dressed you and fed you when we could manage it, even though you were three years old and could do all these things yourself. You did *shishi* on command in the plastic wastebasket since your skinny legs weren't long enough to hit the toilet bowl. We followed your lead by the direction of your finger: empty wastebasket into toilet, rinse with water from tub, flush, wash hands.

By the fourth night, you cried when our mother put you to bed. She sensed you were starting to test her.

WE WOKE at 5:00 a.m. the next day, and by 7:30 we were back at the embassy, this time for our interview, which took place at the booth window. The man behind the glass asked if the boy had any special requirements for his care. Love, our father said. We stayed until late in the afternoon, when we could finally pick up your visa.

Then, on July 10, after our two-week journey, the four of us packed up to leave. Ahead stood twenty-six hours of travel: a cab, three planes, an airporter bus, and another cab. We arrived home Sunday night and the house suddenly looked very different with you in it. You threw your first tantrum shortly after we walked in the door, beating your fists on the carpet.

OUR MOTHER KEPT a stack of adoption literature next to her bed, but it never occurred to me to read any of it as a kid. After a year of trips to the fertility clinic, I asked our mother if I could take some books home. I felt hungry for something austere and impersonal, but many of the texts were written by adoptive mothers for adoptive mothers, often glossy, self-published-looking things with clip art of the Madonna on the front. I opened one called *The Primal Wound: Understanding the Adopted Child* for about five minutes before using it as a leveler for our kitchen table.

So I went back to the library, back to some of the Victorians I loved, the books, you'd say, that you'd use as levelers for your table, and noticed the adoption plot shake out in two ways: (1) the adoptee repairs the state of the family, one broken by the biological children or lack thereof, e.g., the little blond angel who shows up on the doorstep of the town misanthrope in *Silas Marner*, or (2) the adoptee brings chaos and disaster to everyone around them, e.g., Heathcliff in *Wuthering Heights*.

In high school I was tortured by Heathcliff and Cathy's romance but in rereading I was drawn to other things, like the first description of Heathcliff as he walked through the door: *We crowded round, and over Miss Cathy's head I had a peep at a dirty, ragged, black-haired child; big enough both to walk and talk: indeed, its face looked older than Catherine's; yet when it was set on its feet, it only stared round, and repeated over and over again some gibberish that nobody could understand.*

Who had taught him to walk, I wondered. The effect was eerie. How different could life have been if he'd arrived as an infant on the stoop rather than a boy old enough to step over it. I watched Hindley, the biological son, with interest, threatened by the stranger first because of his father's attention, then later because of the question of inheritance. It was strange to me that he was unable to see what was obvious, that Heathcliff could never fall heir to the estate, too cursed by a missing history. That he'd never end up with Cathy for the same reason.

And the names Heathcliff is called. Had I noticed this the last time I read it? *Villain, it, devil, black, black villain, low ruffian, gipsy, unreclaimed, an arid wilderness of furze and whinstone, his countenance a bleak, hilly coal-country.* I'd forgotten that he confesses to Nelly, the housekeeper, his longing for Edgar Linton's light hair, fair skin, and blue eyes, to which Nelly tells him: Who knows, maybe you're actually a prince in disguise. And who could have known this better than you, the way darkness casts it shadow across a white house, a white town, a white life. How you'd asked our mother if you looked like her with your matching brown hair and brown eyes. How you'd asked me if only blond boys were handsome. A peace finally dusts over the house in Heathcliff's absence, only to dispel the moment he returns.

DICKENS'S FATHER was a government clerk who was imprisoned for debt, which sent Dickens to work in a blacking warehouse at the age of twelve, informing some of the experiences later depicted in *David Copperfield*. Sometimes reading him felt like an orphan house of mirrors; half the cast of *Great Expectations* was grappling with the loss of a first family, a history. There's Pip, who renames himself as a child to something he can pronounce on his own, spending the first page of the novel describing the tombstones of his mother and father, the fundamental loss that sends the story on its way. Magwitch, the convict who later financially adopts Pip, is also an orphan who, long ago, named himself as Pip has, in the absence of parents to do it for him. Herbert's wife, Clara Barley, has no mother and hardly any family, a situation from which Herbert is eager to free her. And of course there is the centerpiece of the book, the cold and beautiful ward Estella, adopted by Miss Havisham as a toddler. Estella does not, in her case, bring destruction to the Satis House—destruction already lives there—but instead transmits it back out to the world, intent on ruining all those who cross her path, Pip included. But there is an irresistible old hurt that binds them, traced back to childhood, maybe even an odd relief in each other, that seems to suspend beyond the novel's last sentence.

I wondered when I read it if, in another life, one where you enjoyed reading books, you would feel struck by this connection. It's no coincidence, perhaps, that your bride was, once upon a time, an orphan, too.

MANSFIELD PARK, *Daniel Deronda, Doctor Thorne, Jane Eyre*. Adoption symbolized disruption from a growing industrialism, one text reasoned. It aligned with a common Christian plot structure, said another, where characters were expelled from the Eden of the womb into isolation. But I found England's nineteenth-century divorce legislation the more interesting argument. With family structures breaking down, questions billowed up around legal status for biological and adopted children, and all this inheritance anxiety clawed its way into the literature, in the way that it had with Heathcliff.

There was always poverty, too, and sex, scars left on people both real and imagined. If illegitimate children died without a husband or wife, their personal property passed to the Crown, even if they had been raised in a loving home. They could not take Holy Orders or hold any position of dignity in the Church. There was only one way a child could be legitimated and that was by an Act of Parliament.

BUT I KEPT COMING BACK to Heathcliff, to this primitivism projected onto the bodies of dark, fictional adoptees. The narrative stretched back as far as *The Epic of Gilgamesh*. Enkidu, coated in thick hair, who grazes with the gazelles, is more animal than man before he's adopted by Gilgamesh's mother. He weeps at the knowledge that he was born without family, and is grateful to be taken in, but his own rescue is not the purpose of his plotline: he's been created by the gods to save the people of Uruk from King Gilgamesh's tyranny, and ultimately to save Gilgamesh from himself.

Another feral adoptee appears in Kipling's *The Jungle Book*, the Disney version you loved growing up. Mowgli appears hanging from a branch, just old enough to walk, when adopted by the family of wolves, who bring him to Council Rock to approve his assimilation into the pack. Eventually Mowgli is cast out both by the wolves in the jungle and the men in the village, even after killing the wicked Shere Khan. *I am two Mowglis*, he croons. *My heart is heavy with the things that I do not understand.*

The more I looked, the quicker I found the formula: a family either destroyed or fulfilled, the adoptee ornamenting a sameness or tamed by it, and in this way saved, but perhaps not for long. I thought again of our own family mythology, the way we described our first meeting. Out you walked from the doorway, powder swiped on your face to combat the lice, your frame shaky, unable to speak. This was the story we all participated in, you included, with love and fondness, with each anniversary, every birthday.

Is this not imperialist nostalgia at its best, bell hooks writes, *potent expression of longing for the "primitive"? One desires "a bit of the Other" to enhance the blank landscape of whiteness.* I underlined the question because it troubled me.

EVENTUALLY I PICKED UP *The Primal Wound* again and found myself reading it cover to cover. Our mother had underlined a sentence that said, *The fact that the child does not consciously remember the substitution of mothers does not diminish the impact of that experience.*

I stopped at the page that said, *The people from whom the child steals are likely those whom he respects the most, and there is tremendous reluctance to return that which was stolen, for fear of being returned himself.*

A later chapter stated the FIVE CARDINAL RULES FOR ADOPTIVE PARENTS:

1. NEVER THREATEN ABANDONMENT
2. ACKNOWLEDGE YOUR CHILD'S FEELINGS
3. ALLOW YOUR CHILD TO BE HIMSELF
4. DO NOT TRY TO TAKE THE PLACE OF THE BIRTH MOTHER
5. YOU CANNOT TAKE AWAY YOUR CHILD'S PAIN

I studied the last cardinal rule. Were we capable of taking away our own?

THE NIGHT BEFORE your wedding I fall into strange, lucid dreams. In one, I'm birthing a baby in front of the wedding guests, the crowd watching from their seats; in another you're yelling at me but keep mistaking me for our father, no matter how many times I correct you. In the last, three faceless people are walking you down the aisle; I assume it's us until I notice that one has the head of Peaches, our old garage cat. She walks past me and says, *I persssssssonally would have done things differently.* I spit at her, because I'm certain she means the flowers.

THERE ARE SEVEN INSTANCES of infertility over the Bible's six thousand years, all attributed to women, all of whom conceive sons with the help of God, with the exception of Michal, the first wife of David, who is thought to have died childless. One Sunday in church with our mother, I hear the story of Elkanah and his two wives, Peninnah and Hannah. Every year, Elkanah would go to sacrifice to the Lord at Shiloh, and on the day when he sacrificed, he would give portions to Peninnah and all of her children, but to Hannah he gave double, because he loved her, even though the Lord had closed her womb.

Peninnah, in her cameo, sounded terrible. She provoked Hannah, reminding her that the Lord had closed her womb, as if Hannah needed reminding. So it went on year after year, with Peninnah's cruelty and Hannah still with no children of her own. Hannah wept and would not eat.

Elkanah said to her, Hannah, why do you weep? Why don't you eat? Why is your heart sad? Am I not more to you than ten sons?

One year Hannah decided to go to Shiloh herself, the first woman in scripture to petition the Lord directly. She prayed and wept bitterly. Eli the priest came across her as she prayed and, in seeing her lips moving soundlessly, assumed she was drunk.

How long will you make a spectacle of yourself? Eli said. Put away your wine.

But Hannah told him she was a woman deeply troubled. She had not been drinking but pouring out her soul. She asked not to be regarded as worthless, she had only been speaking out her great anxiety.

Then Eli answered, Go in peace, may God grant the petition you have made to him.

They rose early in the morning and worshipped before the Lord; then they went back to their house at Ramah. Elkanah knew his wife, and the Lord remembered her. In time Hannah conceived and bore a son, whom she named Samuel.

AFTER OUR LUNCH together in the city, something turned for me on the clomiphene treatments. The world became colorless: gray buildings, gray skies, gray trees, as if a plane had crop-dusted the city. This often changed with the dosage; some weeks it turned the world Technicolor instead, bright with rage and injustice, the saturation stinging my eyes. Words were poor indicators of feelings: *manic, sad, hopeless, jealous.* All insufficient. When I heard this passage from Samuel with our mother, a story meant to provide a happy ending, I heard only the words *and the Lord remembered her.* I almost stood up and screamed: *What had she done to be forgotten???*

WHAT'S IT LIKE to be married, you'd asked me, and I never considered how the answer might change. How children had begun to materialize in restaurant windows, spill out from bathrooms, appear behind the library shelves. How trains were filled with pregnant women, creatures I often watched with reverence rather than envy. It wasn't just that they had passed through to the other side, where purgatory would not release me; I was struck, too, by how they took up space, gorgeously, flagrantly, hand on their stomach like a queen with her scepter. *Make way, there's a pregnant lady!* passengers would yell, and I'd wonder if they could just step right through me, my own body waifish, a ghost.

I never considered how guilt could creep through a home. Instead of drawing closer to my husband, the guilt grew between us, because I couldn't let go of the saddest reversal of all: that his goodness, which I had held dear for so long, was now wasted only on me. I wondered if when I first met him, twenty-four and motherhood far from my mind, some part of me had inevitably assessed how his looks might fuse with mine. How his kindness would transfer to more versions of me. Maybe it's not possible to fall in love without this biological valuation of future assets. Though if this were true, then what did he see in me now?

One evening I came home from work and walked into the room we used as an office. I sat on the pullout couch we'd bought for friends and faced him while he sat at his desk. I said the words I'd been rehearsing, that I was tired, that it had become too much, that

I needed a break from the feeling that ran through my body, a certainty that I'd been forgotten, passed over, another pained woman taken for a drunk.

How long? he said.

I looked out the window, where a breeze passed through the sweet gum trees. I knew what he was thinking, how long it would be before I'd want to stop entirely and because I didn't know the answer to that either I said nothing. Instead I sat with the silence between us and wondered if, at one point, the two of us actually would have been enough. I heard Martha's line just before the lights dim. *Just . . . us?*

WE SPENT ONE WEEKEND researching foster and adoption agencies during that break. I thought of how different the process might have looked for our parents as I reviewed the search filters online, with options to sort based on age, race, sex, number of children, or children whose profiles included a video. The fact that I could do this felt both convenient and questionable. It seemed that this method, so far from the experience of pregnancy, should have at least attempted to mirror it, simulating a mixture of chance and fate rather than customization. Instead it was the kind of tailored consumer experience we'd come to expect from the internet, the same demands that filled my workweek. But I also felt a tenderness I hadn't expected as we scrolled through, the smiles either large or awkward; I found myself looking for your frown. I clicked on a few of the children's profiles, which noted their hobbies, their respect for adults, their good attitude despite life's challenges. Most profiles either ended or began with the words *X is looking for a forever family*, a phrase that stayed with me long after the memory of most of the faces disappeared.

I never told our parents this, but I called one of the agencies the following week, spoke to a woman whose voice was gentle. She said that the next step would be to register our family online and then attend the mandatory training workshops.

Do you know about the home-studies process? she asked, and your brother-in-law looked at me as we sat there on speaker and she explained how a social worker would come to our home, ask us questions, take notes. How once we passed we could be matched with a child and from there be on our way to adoption.

ONE SUNDAY AFTERNOON, not long after, our father showed up at my apartment, unannounced. It was midafternoon and I was in my robe.

What are you doing here? I said, and our father actually took a step back from the door. Sorry, I said. Come in.

Our father moved quietly past me, standing with his hands in his pockets in the middle of my living room.

You can sit, I said.

I don't think I'll stay, he said.

I don't know what our mother would have done if it had been her there with me. I just know that our father ran his eyes over the living room, saw the books spread out on the couch, the coffee table, the floor, the paperwork from your box. He asked what I was reading and I told him the truth: a case study about an adoptee from Ukraine who began to threaten his adoptive mother with a knife.

Our father put his hands on my shoulders and said, Get dressed. So I took off my robe and put on my jacket and shoes and then our father walked me three times around the neighborhood. We looked up at the trees and though it saddened me to see them in bloom, the breeze seemed to air out my insides. I thought of how many mornings I'd woken to the sound of his luggage, the keys in his pocket, and run out of bed to catch him, begging to go with him. I asked if he remembered this.

You wore me down, he said. We spent that terrible night in Dallas.

Was it terrible?

You did homework in a conference room all day, and then the two of us went straight to dinner.

I don't remember the dinner.

That was the best part. We expensed everything.

I just remember it was during the tantrums. The day was a vacation.

Not for your mother, he said. Alone with your brother and you missing school. But you're right, you seemed as happy as anything.

I wanted to tell him what else I remembered. That in the morning I'd packed all the little soaps in my suitcase, and from the plane the brown hills of our county seemed to place us in the context of something much larger. I wanted to tell him that what I remembered later, when he would leave again, was not how hard life could be on the road, or the burden of financial responsibility, but the way he could exit when the rest of us couldn't, pulled up into the sky where the problems of a house looked so small. I wanted to tell him that maybe you were right, that I'd taken a job like his so that, on a moment's notice, I could leave home behind.

I WENT BACK on the Clomid, its function to increase the hormones that supported the growth and release of a mature egg. Month after month I would return for my ultrasound, squinting at the follicles on the screen while the nurse measured: right ovary, three millimeters, six millimeters; left ovary, seven millimeters, eight. At twenty millimeters the shot would be injected into my abdomen to induce ovulation but this time I couldn't seem to get any follicles to audition for the lead role. More pills, more hopes, more months, another trip for the ultrasound. Grow, little guys, grow, I would catch myself saying while I walked home, sometimes tenderly, sometimes not. My lips would move with the repetition, like a madwoman, like a drunk.

In those darkest moments, our two bodies worlds away, I would often think of you and feel a connection that I still can't explain. I would think of the way your body would throw itself on the floor, furious, possessed. The mumble you'd make when you were unhappy. *What did you say? Nothing, nothing.* My heart would come back to you in these moments, at 2:00 a.m., 3:00 a.m., 4:00 a.m., while my husband and the city around me slept, and sometimes I'd reach for the phone before some other demon, more stubborn than the rest, would stop me.

I MAGINE: A FIVE-YEAR GESTATION and a twenty-four-pound birth. In the years and months leading up to your arrival, all our parents could do was talk about feelings of expectancy. Now that you were here, the days spoke for themselves.

Petaluma at that time was around 45,000 people, a demographic split between white and Latino, with Asians making up fewer than 3 percent. Though back then it was a sleepy farm town, nestled inland, forty miles north of San Francisco, some outsiders knew it from one of its two previous titles: the Egg Capital of the World and the Arm Wrestling Capital of the World, the former still commemorated with a spring parade and the latter with a statue and fall competition that you and I once attended at the Buffalo Wild Wings. We lived on the west side, near the town's largest church and modest strip of downtown, but no matter where we were—waving at a car in the parking lot of the Petaluma Market, walking by the river that wound south toward the San Pablo Bay—we could always look up to find the hills surrounding us, fortresslike. They were minted green in the winter; in the summer they became big fat women in bed, covered by burlap sacks pulled taut. Our mother had you baptized and, in a few years' time, enrolled in my Catholic school and, as you came to realize, the topographical map of your life became white very suddenly.

Crowds flocked to meet you. All the aunts, uncles, cousins, and grandparents you acquired overnight were fixtures in the house. Our mother's friends from church came by with crucifixes and blessings, my classmates marveled at how impressively different my family was from their own. In fact, when the school year started up again in the fall, my first point of business was to bring you in for fourth-grade show-and-tell. I sat you on a stool and introduced you to forty white faces: this was my brother, and this summer I had traveled to an orphanage in Thailand to bring him home. You sat there politely, perhaps sensing that this was a big moment for me. When it was time for questions, I answered them with ease and authority, until a boy in the back raised his hand. How much did you pay for him? the boy inquired. That's not how it works, I wanted to say, but a shame was already pouring in while our teacher corrected him. You smiled at the boy and in the midst of our audience I tried to understand if I had betrayed you. I took you off the stool and ushered you out to the hallway, where our mother was waiting. I had trouble explaining which of us I was crying for.

NEIGHBORS, FAMILY, teachers, friends: suddenly everyone was all questions.

Was life very different now with the new child? What was he like? Wasn't I happy?

It's good, I'd say, shrugging. He's just my brother, just like anybody having a brother. I wondered why the simplest concepts were so difficult for adults.

But lately I found myself bringing these questions back to our parents; I asked them if the reality was much different from how I remembered it. Was it different? Was I happy?

What were any of us like, our mother said. There was a new baby in the house. We were bewildered. We were happy. We were tired.

Though on the weekdays, she added, you went to school and your father went to work. Often he traveled. I was the one who was home all the time.

WHAT I'VE NEVER BEEN ABLE to describe to you or anyone else is how I meant those words growing up, *He's just my brother*, that you were my blood, my coconspirator, my nuisance, my baby. That you weren't different, some alien, a stranger or freak. I never wanted to talk about otherness because you weren't other to me growing up, you were just my brother, but now I see how one-sided that is.

You were different, after all, in our house, in our school, in our town. I should have figured out ways to talk to you about how you were navigating that difference, a white family, a white life. I should have recognized my own discomfort, misunderstood for love or protection or sparing your feelings. Because how can silence ever be the better, more loving alternative?

LET ME TRY to start again.

When I think of the way I love you, the way I know you, how I might try to describe it, I keep returning to our beginning, those first years together in the house. One would think that given all the hours and days accumulated, there would be much to pick and choose from, but so much becomes lost in the act of living. Ask me now what I remember best about those early years and my answer is the same as our parents': the tantrums.

You were angry, understandably, though we weren't prepared for how you might show it. Here was all this change and no language to ask questions, demand answers. Biologically, you were already at an age where you were supposed to test us, on top of everything else you had on your plate.

But it wasn't all miserable. Some of the things that made you happy right away were swimming pools, ketchup, trains, and the rewind button on the VCR so that you could watch *The Three Musketeers* on repeat. Ay-yah! you'd cry, running through the house with the broom, pointing its round tip at my heart. Finally our mother bought you a plastic sword from Kmart and you became a capable fencer overnight, slashing your weapon left and right along with D'Artagnan on the screen. For your second Halloween, you wore a blue tablecloth, rain boots, a hat with a feather, and tucked your sword into your toddler-size belt. I'd never seen you prouder.

But then you'd remember yourself. I could never account for the sights, sounds, or things denied to you that would bring on the reminder, but a phantom wave would cross your face and drown all the joy that had just been lounging there. Suddenly you'd seem to recall the confusion of your situation, the chains of your body, and, to exorcize the pain, you'd beat those tiny fists: on the floor, on the furniture, on our mother's stomach. You would cry and scream.

GRADUALLY I BECAME RELIEVED when they'd start up at home instead of in public, especially once they became longer, louder, more frequent and difficult to contain; I could at least find solace in the privacy of your pain. The phantom wave could appear at any time, and did: in the cart at Ross Dress for Less, in a silent pew at church. Once it happened in the car in front of school and I slid down in my seat so that none of my classmates would associate me with the terrible sound of you.

I don't remember any of that, you used to say. You don't remember how the sound of your pain had incredible range. It always seemed to be retuning itself, finding limitless ways to unsettle you, and us. To say *scream* is actually misleading, implying a single note carried through, on-key in a horror film. From your mouth the devil, with his untrained ear, played all his instruments, stamping a cloven hoof on the pedals of the piano while his elbow banged the keys, his singing voice like microphone feedback, fingers strumming a chalkboard.

Our parents started putting you in your room when it happened; sometimes they'd sit in there with you, waiting for up to an hour for you to cool off. Once I ran in and screamed, Shut up, shut up, shut up! but was scolded by our mother and didn't do it again. I would hear you in there, the sounds rising, shriller, the orchestra pouring from your mouth, while your face was soaked in sweat, tears, and snot. And in the later months, I'd hear the trajectory of tiny trains, tiny shoes, more tiny fists, end against the door. It was impossible to remember anymore the quiet of the house before you had come; I could hear you wherever I went. Often when the noise settled down I'd come in to find you asleep in the detritus, your room and your little body a wreck. You'd awake later, staring blankly, as if you'd left yourself during the incident and were unable to tell me what had happened.

OUR MOTHER saved copies of the home studies from Rosemary Pascal, the social worker who continued to visit us every few weeks once you came home. These reports were faxed back to the agency for the first six months. They sat among your paperwork like entries torn from a stranger's notebook, the four of us sketched like paper dolls. *The mother enjoys childrearing. The father works in sales. The children like to play basketball. The Larsens live in a rented house and remain in good health.*

I don't remember much about her, our mother said, except that whenever she came I got nervous. She was always inspecting the windows and outlets.

This afternoon I drove to the west side of town to visit the family in their home. The street is safe and quiet. The house itself was tidy. The family was sitting in the backyard, where Daniel was eating an apple from the tree. Some of his new words and phrases are: up, this way, more, so handsome.

I never knew how much to clean, our mother said.

He's a smart boy, very compassionate, too. When his sister was crying about something, he went over to her and put his little arms around her to console her.

Crying? our mother said. I wish I remembered more. The beginning was so hazy.

Say, then, that Rosemary lived on the east side of town, past the old Tuttle Drugs, past the drawbridge and the brick silk mill, out by the municipal airport, where we used to go to the Two Niner Diner on special occasions to watch the planes fly in. It might have been a twenty-minute drive to our house. Say that Rosemary woke up to her own family, two kids already at the table, their heads in their breakfast, without a thought for how they might look as they sat there together, what their conversation might have signaled, what could be said about the way they handled their spoons. Rosemary kissed her husband goodbye and did not consider how her own home would hold up under scrutiny. Instead she walked into our yard to find a similar scene: two kids outside eating breakfast. The older one would go to school late and the father would take the morning off so that they could complete the tableau vivant. It was September, and in a month this beautiful weather would change, but this morning the family looked as though they always took their breakfast outside. She asked the parents about life with a new toddler. *He eats like a horse,* the father said, which didn't sound like something he'd say at all, and I wondered if Rosemary, in transcribing the scene later, allowed herself a few artistic liberties. The mother reminded Rosemary that the boy had three parasites when he arrived home, but that was all treated now. Rosemary asked the young girl about the changes at home, and she said that she loved being a sister. The boy moved to his mother's lap. *Daniel had kicking, screaming temper tantrums when he was first placed but those have diminished, he is much better able to express himself now.*

Oh no, said our mother. They went on for months after that.

He eats like a horse, says his father! She took a few steps back and snapped our photo. *Enclosed are the pictures requested. He feels very much at home; he has adjusted beautifully.*

YOU WERE ALWAYS BRINGING SOMETHING into the house: some disaster, metaphoric or literal, tragic or comic. Once, on a comprehensive search through the suitcases in the garage, a task that served no concrete purpose, you brought one small piece of luggage into the kitchen to show our mother. No, no, she began to scold, because the suitcases brought in cat hair from the outdoor male stray you and I called Peaches. We'd crack the garage door at night so Peaches could sleep in the suitcases next to the cat bed. As our mother began to wheel the suitcase back to the garage you said you'd brought it in because you had something to tell her. There was something soft inside, you said, and then our mother followed your lead and opened it.

You didn't begin screaming until she did; it wasn't until her shrill cries registered in your ears that you realized something was terribly wrong. Out ran the baby opossum, blinded by the cruel light of the afternoon, clearly in a place he didn't belong, so far from the dark cover of the luggage. The opossum waddled its way through the kitchen, the den, hanging a left into the laundry room, and then our mother collected herself enough that she was able to follow its horrible rodent tail through the house. How could you have screwed up so badly by showing off what you had found? You cried. And our mother did her best to soothe you, picked you up, and ran outside to find the man who had been hired that afternoon to paint the porch.

Help, our mother cried. She cried the words for both of you. And the porch painter became an unexpected hero that afternoon while our father was away on business, as he pushed the washing machine from the wall so our mother could gently whack the tush of the little creature with the broom, spanking it out the back door, where it scuttled, gratefully, into the cool cloak of the bushes.

Then, of course, there was the crow, but you'll argue that one wasn't your fault. You simply heard scratching in the chimney and opened the flue. And coming down for breakfast, I discovered our mother running through the house, broom raised high over her head, as she tried to spank that creature out, too. This time, rather than crying, you sat on the couch, mouth open, eyes fixed on the crazed black bird. It was either trying to free itself or find its place against the walls of the living room, though which we couldn't seem to say.

SOMETIMES I WONDER if your first memories turn on right after that trip to Disneyland. Perhaps it was the paper plates of steaming french fries, the star power of Mickey Mouse, the hotel pool. It made a deep impression. If it hadn't already been deemed the Happiest Place on Earth, you would have invented an equally joyous tagline. There's a photo of your first ride on the teacups, shoulders hunched, knuckles nearly made white by your grip, and those teeth flashing. Everything about you says you are alive and thankful to be. There's an autographed photo of you and Mickey, in which you

stand shyly next to his red trousers. Incidentally, none of us can recall any tantrums occurring in our three days there.

When we came home from that trip, language truly began to
find you, and you reported back that french fries were now your
favorite food; you confessed your unabashed love for the large male
mouse. Either in solidarity or heartsickness you watched a Disneyland musical on loop, songs that haunted me in deep dreams. When
people asked where you were from, you now happily provided them
with an answer. Disneyland, you said.

JULY 4 became an important day in our calendar, the anniversary
of the day we met. All the books our mother read instructed us to
celebrate the anniversary date, to make an occasion, especially the
first few years.

Those first anniversaries were wonderful, actually, almost better than Christmas, because we would drive you to the top of Sun-
crest Hill, where my best friend lived, a spot that provided the best
views over Petaluma, before the new developments came in. We
would park at the top and open the sunroof so that you and I could
poke our heads out. The sun would go down and we'd forget the
hot day and pull on our sweatshirts. And as we watched the colors
come up from the town and into the sky, I would tell you that the
fireworks were for you. Look, I'd say, and you'd look. I'd tell you
that everyone was celebrating that you were here. And you'd stare
up with your eyes big and your little mouth hanging open, as if you
couldn't believe your good luck.

OF COURSE THERE WERE the strange things, too, like the interest
you took in sweeping when you first arrived home, the deep con-
centration that appeared as you directed the broom like a dance

partner, innocent enough to be labeled endearing. There he goes, I'd say, as you'd take off for the dust bunnies in the corner. Occasionally I would lead you around the kitchen, the bathroom, opportunistically ticking off items on my chore list.

Until one morning when our mother took you with her to work. The toilet had overflowed in the office and the janitor left out his bucket and sponge while he went outside for a smoke. Our mother came around the corner to find you with the wet sponge in your hand, rubbing precise circles along the wall. You hadn't yet turned four, and from there the joke turned sour.

I can admit to you now that in the fog of day-to-day living, I sometimes forgot that there was so much we were missing from those first three years of your life. At times it seemed an amount impossible to measure, all the secrets you could never explain to us.

WHERE'S PAPA *going with that ax?* asks Fern in *Charlotte's Web.* You were unsure about Wilbur's story when I read it to you, maybe because it always opened in the same, ominous way, with Mr. Arable walking through the wet morning grass, a weapon in his hand. Maybe because for Wilbur the first hour of life was already uncertain, while the rest of the young pigs spent a few seasons growing fat by their mother's side. I would skip to the part where he's taken in by eight-year-old Fern, who nurses Wilbur on a bottle and wheels him around the farm in a baby carriage, until he's sold to Fern's uncle for six dollars. By the time Wilbur reaches Mr. Zuckerman's farm, we would both be anxious, wondering: Who will tend to the little pig now?

Then Charlotte would appear, full of charm, wit, and courage, transforming from friend to maternal figure overnight. Wilbur's mother, we were always left to assume, still lived with the other piglets on the Arable farm. Wilbur never asked about where he came from, but always worried about who would protect his future. You had no patience for the ending, I remember, asking why all Charlotte's children had to fly away.

There was one book our mother never read with you, given to us by a friend from church, the story of Stellaluna, the fruit bat. Stellaluna and her mother are out searching for food one night when suddenly they're attacked by an owl and separated. A family of birds takes Stellaluna in, but under the condition that she puts her bat habits aside. In fact, Mama Bird threatens to kick her out of the nest if she doesn't start acting like a better bird. So she learns to sleep rightside up and eat bugs without making faces. How can we be so different and feel so much alike, one of the baby bird siblings asks her. And how can we feel so different and be so much alike? says another.

One day while flying, Stellaluna is separated from her adoptive siblings and comes across her bat family. This is the happy ending: the young bat returns with relief to her biological family.

I REMEMBER sitting in the pew with you at church, trying to pray to a holy mother and father, and feeling the great burden of having to love another set of parents, ones only known to us through the wild stories we learned in school. Water to wine, a miraculous conception, resurrection from the dead—it was all impressive but how could it possibly translate to love? How could we feel loyalty to a guardian who'd never physically shown up in our own lives to earn it? Sometimes, while we prayed the Hail Mary with our teacher, I would try to summon our mother's face in case this other mother was trying to crowd ours out. I confessed this to our mother one night, and she said that it was okay to love a mother on earth and a mother in heaven. But it was no comfort at all, being asked to cut love down the center. I wonder if similar questions have troubled your heart from time to time.

I was always worrying from a young age that our mother would die on me, and then on us. She often existed as a voice-over in my head, ruling on the good and poor decisions that occurred when we were apart. This continued when I was older—when riding to a bar once in the trunk of a car, when going home with a stranger. I'm sorry, I would say, the prayer earthbound, and ask her to avert her eyes. Sometimes, when I didn't hear her, I would feel certain that she was hurt or in a coma, that something had happened to sever the connection. Maybe when she was really gone, I thought, I would finally be able to love the other mother equally. But then our mother would probably just outshine everybody in heaven. Because when she leaned in to kiss us, there was the scent of the rose soap that she kept in her drawers, and all the jewelry on her body would chime with the motion, like the little bells that rang during the consecration—the long earrings, the medals around her neck, the two small gold bracelets our father had given her—chime, chime, chime, as if something sacred were happening.

SHE USED TO HAVE that funny saying; we would whisper it back and forth, rolling our eyes. When bad stories would pop up in the news or in gossip around the table, our mother would say at the end, *And that's why you have to be kind to each other.* As if kindness was the dividing line from the killers, the key to a happy and productive life. The *each other* was you and me.

There was such an age difference between us that we never really physically fought, except for that time you were mad and jabbed me in the arm with a pencil, deep enough that it drew blood. I cried out and hit you across the face. I think we were both surprised at the sound it made, a thud, rather than the crisp slap of the movies. I don't know that we were kinder to each other after that, but maybe we were a little more careful.

THESE DAYS IT might surprise your bride to know that you were once the boy who would have done anything to get out of church. Laundry, homework. For a while you were allowed to bring in trucks or coloring books, but as you got older these distractions were forbidden and you would sigh audibly, head thrown up to the heavens, as if the hour was the longest in your life.

Most of the time I understood; it's difficult to feel awe over a routine part of life. Our weeks at school were filled with prayers before first period, prayers before lunch, confession and Communion on Fridays, the sacraments crowding into our weekends, too. But as a kid I loved the rich blue of the robe that the priest wore during advent, appearing just days before Petalumans began stringing their houses with lights. I loved the way his voice would build itself up, decibel by decibel, over the course of a sermon. I loved when he would pass through the aisles with the aspergillum and a hundred signs of the cross would wave through the church. You confided in me that you didn't like church but you liked the music, though this was hardly a secret. You'd stand up from the floor and peer over the pew and watch the choir in a kind of trance, often humming along. I didn't love all the songs we sang, but there were a handful that would sometimes make me want to cry for no reason, and still do.

By high school you stopped going, to the disappointment of our mother. On Sunday mornings you would disappear from the house, heading to either the park or the gym to make sure you couldn't be tricked into changing your mind. Though I do remember you showing up once: a morning during our mother's cancer. I was twenty-three and alone in the pew, there to collect the host to bring home to her, and suddenly you appeared beside me. You'd come for me, though you didn't say it. I will never forget that kindness, or the comfort I felt at the sight of you. You didn't kneel when it was time to kneel, but you sat through the whole mass quietly, your shoulder pressed against mine.

WHEN DID YOU LEARN to hide things from me? Why can't we go back to that story I always tell, you five or six years old, your smile sly as you placed my wrapped gift under the tree. *MERRY CHRSMTMAS LOVE DANNY LARSEN.*

What did you get me for Christmas, Danny? I'd teased.

Not slippers, you'd said.

WHEN DID I LEARN to hide things from you?

I ONCE READ love defined as a refusal to think of someone in terms of power. I'd never considered love in this context, in the context of power, and in that way the definition felt far from me, even though in theory I practiced it. After all, your brother-in-law and I had shared everything from the beginning. Keys and friends and a perpetual cold. A degree and its corresponding ambitions, and shame for those ambitions. A coffee grinder and a pan and a pot and a horrible sweatshirt with a psychedelic wolf. Money, even, right away, because neither of us had much to keep tabs on. Staying in love seemed as simple as the words themselves, a matter of keeping put someplace happy.

But power structures don't cease to exist just because two people refuse them, and now I think this definition holds less weight. To try to forget power in the name of love is only a sacrifice from the person who lacks it.

What feels true is this: problems in a marriage result from a shift in the balance, a disruption in some unspoken agreement upon which happiness has been built. Maybe a child always tipped the scales, triggering one person's rise or descent. Whatever I had lost of myself in the process, though, hadn't seemed to transfer to my husband. So where did the power go then? Who ascended? What if nobody did?

ONE NIGHT at a party, pumped full of hormones, I spotted your brother-in-law talking to a woman. Her hands were thrust coolly in her pockets, as if pinning her otherwise weightless frame to the earth. Her shoulders were pulled back and her hair was pulled back and everything about her seemed open, switched on, electric with sex, and I tried to remember the last time I'd done anything that wasn't instigated by my calendar. I looked at this person and recalled an evening last month when, in our small window of procreational hope, I'd been so sure I was getting strep throat that we decided to go through it without kissing, bearing it bravely, civilly, mechanically, like two virgins obliged to their wedding night. And probably it should have been funny, stumbling around the body I knew best—*Sorry, this way, did you? Good night*—trying not to get him sick, but I realized that in the old days he wouldn't have minded sickness at all, that he would have put his hands and mouth in a hundred different places and taken sickness without thinking, because back then we shared everything, because back then we touched each other with a different desperation, and I looked at this person and I looked at my husband and I became so tired of it that I walked out the door. On the street I ran the five blocks to the train and when I boarded my heart was beating so loudly I wondered if the stranger next to me could hear it. My phone rang halfway through the ride, and when I answered with satisfaction that I was almost home, it was my husband's confusion that brought me back, and I stopped hearing myself and instead heard only the amazement in his voice. *You . . . left?*

In that moment, my anger seemed tied to the evening's events. It was hard to see that back then that same anger fueled everything, burning up even the smallest of trials. Because if you were always angry, how could you distinguish the heat of one perceived injustice from another? I was furious with the commute, with the perpetual clog in the tub, with an imaginary child who had become too stubborn, with a husband who'd remained physically unchanged. I was furious with myself, that there were so many other desires that comprised my personhood but somehow I had been boiled down to this, this chemically altered creature. In the dark window of the train I saw someone else, a monster, subhuman, subwoman, a contaminant, and when I got home an hour passed, and then another, and then another, until finally I heard the key, the toothbrush, the slump into the bed. I knew that in the morning I would apologize and that he would forgive me, but the thing about marriage is that certain fights leave their marks, the permanent stains on one's record, the wife who left her husband behind.

Maybe that time was less about anger and more about an affliction of possibility, the feeling that if I just held on a little longer . . . But how long could a body live in the almost of that space?

I didn't know how to talk about any of it, Danny. Nobody around me knew, either, because silence is the accepted consolation for so many things, and so the isolation grew. The calls stopped coming, a close friend neglected to tell me she was pregnant. Nobody asked anymore if I was still trying, as if it would remind me of something I'd forgotten. As if, monster that I was, my curse would somehow transmit to them.

THE FIRST RECORD of the infertile woman was the lion-headed demoness Lamashtu, in the eighteenth century BCE. The story went that the gods flooded the earth while at war with men. Upon restoring humankind, they introduced a third group of people, who would prevent the world from ever overpopulating again.

Enter Lamashtu, who, barren and envious, roamed around causing infertility, miscarriage, and infant death. Apparently she could be warded off only by reciting all seven of her names.

I DIDN'T MISCARRY; we were never baited with a positive test. One afternoon a nurse said she spotted a promising follicle. This one is a very nice size, she said, very promising, and I practically ran home to tell my husband. We readied the disinfectant, the shot, the sex, and in the two weeks that followed, I practiced a kind of catholic abstinence. No white flour, no alcohol, no tight clothing, no exercise. I jogged across the street to catch the light one evening without thinking and then repented the rest of the way home.

And the world looked different again, except this time it all seemed to point toward a yes. I could feel it in the way strangers looked at me on the train, in the rare heat that was pressing into the evenings, as if the strangers knew something I didn't, as if the heat nursed from a life that now whirred within me. I could feel it in my body. *Don't get your hopes up too much*, someone had said, and I didn't know how to answer, I didn't know where exactly my hope was by then. I just understood that it was an impossible thing to ask of a person, of a person who still wanted to live, who was covetous of life.

So the days passed and I hoped and I slept. I slept a kind of beautiful sleep that I'd lost since I was a teenager. The bed returned as a place of comfort and I dove into it like a vast, warm ocean, in which sleep was one long, continuous float.

It was still dark the morning I took the test; I checked the time and went into the bathroom, closed the door. My husband was sleeping and I wanted it that way. I peed and waited and picked up the stick and even then I told myself it could be a mistake. New stick, dribble, wait, same mistake. I went back to bed and knew that my husband was now awake. The sheets were cold and I faced away from him. And this is the hardest thing to explain, but I mourned the loss of that follicle so deeply, that pathetic, nothing, fluid-filled sac. I wondered who, in another's body, with another's luck, that follicle could have been.

I started traveling more frequently for work, bumping into myself in the hotel mirror. Sometimes when I called home I'd feel certain that my husband wouldn't answer, that he'd be at the bar down the street, talking to women who didn't make him feel lonely. But he always did.

L ANGUAGE always seemed to be the great current you were working against and, to fight it, you began picking up words of untraceable origin, lending your own meaning, explaining them to us as if you lived with a household of idiots. There was the period where you created a pejorative out of the word *biscuiter*. It made you seem like some miniature play actor, flinging Shakespearean insults across the stage, ones that made a modern-day audience laugh while scratching their heads. Where did you pick this word up, one who biscuits?

Our father had a theory that the word was a warping of busk. He thought it was something you'd heard on the street, though our mother was skeptical: the number of actual buskers in our suburban town was minimal.

What does that mean, I'd cry at the table each time you hurled the word at me.

A beggar, you once said darkly, only leaving me more confused.

BY KINDERGARTEN you found your first love, a girl with hair the color of corn husks. You followed her around school as you had done with our mother those first days in the hotel.

Maybe language fell like a boulder, blocking the path for all those feelings to come through. Maybe you didn't know how to tell her you thought she was beautiful, how to ask her to be your friend. I just know that instead of throwing yourself on the ground, calls began to come in from her mother, the principal, asking to put an end to the harassment. The crime itself was loosely defined, left to the testimony of five-year-olds. How, in turn, was our mother supposed to communicate this to you? And would those calls still have come, our mother wondered, if your features were light like hers, too?

But I didn't do anything, you said. We sat on the floor of my room, both of us cross-legged on the carpet. It didn't occur to me then that we wouldn't always be like that, just a knock away.

I WATCHED YOU once with a group of boys after soccer practice; I was across the field and couldn't hear the conversation, which is what made me notice how you'd taught yourself to talk with your body. You pulled on the shirts of the boys you liked, attaching to them like a superfluous limb, pushing others away.

That's just boys' stuff, our father said.

Eventually our parents sent you for those speech and language evaluations; you'd gotten in trouble with the principal for calling him *dude*. He thought it was funny, you said, and I'd marveled a little at your guts. But our parents were growing concerned; similar complaints had been cropping up from coaches and teachers about the way you addressed them.

The speech therapist came back with a phrase that I'd begin to hear often in our home, *central auditory processing deficits*. These could be common for children who'd experienced deprivation of sound and language in a critical language period, she said. What kind of interactions had he had in the orphanage? Our mother always gave the same answer: she wished more than anything that she knew. Regular speech therapy was recommended.

I remember at one point our mother set up a playdate with one of the adopted children from Mexico, but you preferred a classmate named Nick, who lived up the road in a house with a big swimming pool. You spent a good deal of time over there for at least a year until one day the invites stopped coming; our mother followed up with phone calls, but couldn't seem to get an answer on what had happened. You also didn't have an explanation.

You and I ran into him a few months later downtown, as he was crossing the street with another friend. You waved and as I watched his mouth tighten into a smirk an insane anger blazed in my chest. *What the fuck is so funny?* I screamed, and he scurried away. You looked up at me. I can't remember if you were impressed or horribly embarrassed, only that my heart raced the rest of the afternoon.

AT THE SAME TIME you were growing so strong. On the weekends, reprieved from his city job and long commute, our father would take us to the park across the street. From the garage you would pull out all the necessary equipment: baseball gloves, soccer balls, Frisbees, bats. But the three of us inevitably wound up on the blacktop because the Bulls were on TV and because at that time I had serious ambitions to play in the WNBA.

Watching you dribble was like watching someone run through a bounce house with a hot beverage. You'd trip down the court and make our father laugh and laugh. Then you'd astonish him by using the same wobbly hands to chuck the ball up to the net, six feet over your head, and sink it. Our father made no secret of his admiration.

Many years later, when I'd return for a weekend from college, you and I would still find ourselves at the blacktop, usually within an hour of my coming home. It was the way for us to make up for lost time, become comfortable around each other's bodies again. By then you were better than me, short but fast. I'd blink and you'd be five feet behind me, sinking a layup. I was impressed but I kept this from you because you were happier when I looked upset. Sometimes we'd just shoot around, and sometimes we'd play in silence, without keeping score.

Travel, you'd say, whenever I made it.

Travel, nice shot.

That would have been great if you hadn't walked ten feet first.

Did you forget in this game you have to dribble?

Once when I was guarding you I noticed scrapes on your hands and knees.

It's nothing, you said, slapping the ball from my hand.

Sometimes I'd ask if you wanted to transfer to another school, how often kids picked on you, if you'd told Mom and Dad, or anyone.

I'm fine where I am, you'd say, all your angers and sorrows locked up, along with all the other things I didn't know about.

WHEN WE WERE YOUNGER I'd ask you: What's your earliest memory? Nine times out of ten you'd play back the Christmas afternoon when I let you drive in three circles around the Safeway parking lot. Our mother had been so busy with the presents that she'd forgotten to buy anything for dinner, and when you and I went out in search of groceries, we found the parking lot empty. It had been my idea to switch seats.

You can go a little faster, I'd said. You don't need your blinker here.

Let's not tell Mom about this, you'd said, as if it made the moment that much happier.

That was Christmas 2001, I would say, which put you at ten.

But what is your *earliest* memory, I'd say. You'd shrug. Perhaps you were offering the first ten years as a gift, out of laziness, out of love, a permission to write all the memories inside them.

THERE'S A FAMOUS STORY in our family, a founding story of sorts, one our mother would often reference with our aunt. Our great-grandfather on our mother's father's side, Peter Marino, was a dyer and his wife, our great-grandma Josephine, was a seamstress. They lived in Brooklyn and money was tight; they had recently emigrated from Naples and had our grandfather and his three siblings to feed. Peter dominated the household with his bad temper. He cranked at the children and he cranked at his wife, passing his particular brand of unhappiness down to his oldest son. Nothing was spent without going through him first, and even approved purchases were met with disdain. Then one evening, without explanation, Peter came home with a mandolin. And the story goes that Josephine took one look at it, picked it up, and crashed it over his head, and from that moment the crown passed, and Grandma Josephine ruled the house.

Our mother says there was a moment like this in our home, a story you've probably heard but would be too young to remember. It happened in 1995 while I was at school and our father at work, and the morning was off to this kind of start: you were kicking and screaming and thrashing so loudly on the floor that even after our mother decided to take you to Happy Day Preschool across town, it still took her thirty minutes to get your writhing body in the car.

The parking lot was empty when you pulled in, and our mother realized that Happy Day was, on this unhappy day, closed. And you began to cry again in your car seat, and our mother began to cry in the front seat, and the two of you wept together in the empty parking lot, the whole sunny day ahead of you.

Our mother took you back home, and you threw yourself back on the kitchen floor, crying and screaming and thrashing again, picking up almost exactly where you'd left off. Our mother took a seat next to you on the floor. And watching you she said finally, I can't do this anymore, Danny; she spoke your name in a voice she'd never used with you. Stop for a moment to look at her here, on the floor. I can see her so clearly on the old linoleum that used to drive her crazy, revealing all the dirt tracked in from the side door. She looks so young to me sitting there, short hair, long earrings, no shoes. She had already raised one child but the rules had changed from first to second—a guilt often pressed in when she scolded you, reprimanded you, and now she could see that it was her guilt that kicked your legs up in the air, made you beat the ground with your fists. It clicked. And, as has always been the case, she was first to understand you.

No more, she said to the guilt.

No more, Danny, she said to you.

You looked back at her curiously, as if considering the weight of that crown, a power that had burdened your small, shaky frame. The tears died down. And you followed her around the rest of the day, questioning, questioning, and until the sun went down every answer she gave you was no. That was the last of the tantrums there on the kitchen floor, where the crown passed. After everything, you seemed to retire it with relief.

MAYBE A FAMILY stripped down to its roots is just a shared story, all translations traced back to an original source. This might explain how it felt when that story went missing, with an estrangement, with a death, pieces of history that dissolved when no longer passed back and forth. How disorienting it was.

What would become of the story, years from now, if neither of us picked up the phone to remember?

WHEN WE WERE GROWING UP our mother would kiss us and say, *My life didn't begin until I had you.* It made me angry and for a long time I couldn't figure out why. I think I wanted her to claim what had been before us; I wanted her to claim a life beyond being our mother.

If I had a daughter, I would try to explain all the beginnings there could be. Or maybe I would look in her face and understand what our mother was probably trying to say. That, in seeing her there, the other beginnings ceased to matter.

B Y JUNIOR HIGH, teachers were calling you angry, and our parents sent you to therapy. You were getting into fist-fights and still attending speech-and-language sessions a few hours a week. The school had put you in a Friendship Group.

What's a Friendship Group? I asked.

It's a new thing, our mother said.

It's stupid, you said. Can't they at least call it something less stupid?

He's not wrong, I said to our mother.

After the first session the therapist called. You had trouble completing tasks, paying attention, and keeping organized, she reported. Our mother had listened, wondering if this was the great revelation she was paying for. Recently during an exam you had quit midway and put your head on the table, closing your eyes over your test paper.

What do you think of her?

Who?

The therapist.

I don't know. She's white.

Our mother shuttled us from appointment to appointment, until soon I was driving and then she just shuttled you. This is a place where the narrative splits again, each of us setting off into the wildernesses of junior high and high school. I had my own reasons for being angry, I was gangly and A-cupped and covered in acne, but I could hide in the crowds at a time when it hurt to stick out. It was a relief to slip into the landscape, to erase myself. It was a relief that I could do it.

I remained unaware of so much that was going on with you then, all the degradations of your school day, too caught up in my own. I just knew there was always some drama when you came home, a fight, another stern phone call from a parent or teacher. There was the afternoon the principal called because you'd paid a girl to walk twice around the track, holding your hand.

PEOPLE WERE ALWAYS TELLING YOU how much better off you were in America.

Who? Other kids?

The moms, you'd say. Always the moms for some reason.

Thailand was very hot. Thailand was very poor. Thailand was very far away. No Big Macs there, someone said to you, which was untrue.

A classmate asked if you missed your mother.

No, you said, I'll see her later.

No, dummy, he'd said. Your birth mother.

He's the dumb one, I'd said when you told me.

I know, you said, but you looked unconvinced.

I don't remember, anyway.

You don't remember what you said?

No. I don't remember her.

I looked at you and waited.

It's stupid, you said, and shook your head. Because I can't

remember. You said this as if it were a joke. How can I miss her if I can't remember?

WHEN YOU'D HAD A REALLY BAD WEEK at school, when the basketball court wasn't enough, our father would take us to Best Buy. You loved it there—something about the shiny yellow signs and scent of electronics would transform you, as you'd count and recount the cash in your pocket from your small weekly allowance. One weekend we took you there for your birthday because you had two gift cards and your head was full of plans: you scanned the aisles hungrily until finally deciding on an MP3 player. But our father explained that the value of the cards didn't match the price of the item, and that you'd have to wait and save or pick out something else. Your whole body grew rigid, your eyes cast at the floor, and I wondered for a moment if you were going to have a tantrum for the first time in almost a decade.

Then I'll take these, you said, grabbing headphones from the rack, almost at random. You have headphones, our father said, but you insisted. At the register you came up short with the money; the cashier said that one of the gift cards had already been spent. How? I said, and the same cloud passed over your body, more darkly this time. Our father looked at the long line behind us and handed over his credit card to cover the difference. You said nothing. Back in the car you cradled the bag while our father explained how installments worked, how you would pay him back over the next few weeks with cash from your allowance. I watched him take the receipt from his pocket and write carefully on the back the letters *IOU*.

AS PUBERTY STRUCK, your looks confused the girls and made the boys manic with envy: your skin stayed smooth; your nose fit your face; you developed a very suave move where you'd brush all the long hair out of your eyes without using your hands. You found cross-country and muscles popped out of your boyish frame overnight.

One day after school you came home and asked if you were a nigger. I can't remember how old you were; I only remember the feeling the question produced, as if you had brought the opossum back into the house again, except that this time it was dead, maggot-filled, and you held it bloodied in your arms, offering it up.

Our mother retrieved the name of the person who might have given you this idea, and immediately called the principal while I stood with you in the kitchen. I was in high school then and didn't know what to say. Maybe language was the current we were all working against, not just you. We were all trying to find our way through it or, on the worst days, around it.

What did you say? I asked.

I told him I was a chink, you said.

HOW SHOULD A FAMILY TALK about this when talk so often felt like a stampede, flattening the answers. We didn't know how to combat the racism that ran through our town, trampled into our home. Despite the counselors, the conferences, the paperwork, the questions we asked you directly, it was hard to understand how feelings got processed. And even though we loved one another, we'd return to our separate corners to cope. In time I moved out to college, our parents called more professionals, and you found the addiction that would follow you into adulthood. What would our friend Rosemary have said of us then.

SOMEHOW, by fifteen or sixteen, you discovered that money could brighten a bad day, and I'm guessing by then you had many. I was out of the house, the information funneled selectively through you and our parents on the phone.

There's still so much I don't understand about this, how it's always isolated action and consequence in your mind. When you took our father's credit card and bought yourself a new bike off the internet, for example, you didn't seem to consider the inevitable response when the bill arrived, or when our mother noticed you taking a joyride on something she hadn't purchased. There was only the feeling of it in your hands when it arrived: happiness, I supposed. Maybe as you rubbed your fingers over its surface it dispelled the bad names and the girl problems and the distress of being invisible in a world where you only stuck out. The bike was the first of the offenses, as far as I remember or was told, and the high must have been like nothing else. You rode around the block and perhaps only then did the long day at high school become a distant memory. Then the bill came and our mother noticed the bike in the garage. A shock resonated through the house and you were punished, though the bike stayed where it was, next to the Christmas decorations.

How much longer was it before the laptop? Months, maybe. Weeks. When our mother discovered it in your room, you told her that it was on loan from school. Our mother couldn't really imagine the town's public high school loaning out new laptops, but the truth was so ludicrous that she chose to believe the lie.

What's remarkable is that you did nothing to prevent the rest of the cycle from occurring. The bill came, announcing a charge for the same device that now sat on the desk in your room. Our mother's voice reached an octave that I hadn't known it could; our father's voice became very, very low. It was a big expense for our parents and when they tried to return it, it was too late. So they donated it to a local charity, perhaps in hopes of dispelling the eeriness in the house that had suddenly replaced the shock.

Why? I said over the phone. Do any of your friends have their own computers?

No, you said. You didn't offer an answer.

THEN OUR MOTHER GOT SICK and it was as if the universe ceased to move; because how could the earth possibly summon the strength for its rotation with our mother stuck upstairs in her bed. Later, we would try to forget how she looked that year: cheeks sunk in, all the color drained from her rosy nose. The hair loss around the back of her head and neck. The new color of her skin, how it turned from a robust Italian bronze to the color of hospital bedsheets. And that awful feeding tube in her stomach, like an umbilical cord. The way her sweatpants suddenly billowed.

I took comfort in you in those months. You understood what it was to see our mother weak, brought to her knees by something invisible. You were someone who didn't need it explained. And I think you needed me, too, because it was the one time in our lives when we spoke every day on the phone. I was living and working in San Francisco, driving home on the weekends, and we would talk each other through Mondays, Tuesdays, Wednesdays, and Thursdays, the calls often containing no questions. *Hi*, you would say. *She just fell asleep again. Okay*, I would say. *I'm just sitting here.* I'd hear the microwave beep or the TV come on. *Same.* You were mad at the doctors for not catching it sooner, you'd tell me. Our mother had asked you to pray and sometimes you did and sometimes you didn't because God seemed more to blame than anything. *How do you pray?* you'd ask. *I don't know*, I would say honestly, *I just beg in my head.* You were mad at the abstractions, the chemo that left her unable to finish a sentence, and I'd tell you I understood because I did. Sometimes I would read from *The Maltese Falcon* and our mother would have to tell me to stop, she couldn't keep up with all those words stacked in a row. TV produced the same problem. What did she want to do? I would ask. Just sit, our mother would say. It frightened you and me terribly, that faraway look that developed from the treatments. It banished all the awareness that joy requires, it seemed to sweep her soul out along with the bad cells.

WE WANDERED around the house zombielike, as if we'd ingested the treatments, too. On Sundays I'd go to mass to receive a consecrated host from the priest to bring back to our mother; you drove her to appointments on the days our father couldn't work from home, helped administer drinks and pills. In that way the time was harder for you. You were the one, after all, who was home with her. I would hug you goodbye Sunday night and often think of you instead of our mother as I drove away. Once or twice I called you from the car and you picked up on the first ring.

One day we freed ourselves from the house, which had become a museum, all the hung pictures curating a time before. We took that long bike ride in the Putnam hills. Neither of us spoke while we pedaled, breathing in our town's contradictions: the dry heat interrupted by Pacific wind, the scents of parched grass and damp oak groves. I began pedaling a little faster, and you went faster, too. Toward the bottom of a hill my tire snagged and I flew off my bike in the middle of the path. A moment later I heard you swerve to try to avoid me, instead landing right on top of my back.

We lay for a few moments, not speaking.

Danny? I said, turning my head.

We must have looked like a crime scene, and from under the

wheel I reached for your arm. I'm okay, you said, rolling off me slowly. I'm okay. You're bleeding, though.

I put a hand to my face and then saw my red fingers. Is anything broken, you think? I said.

No, I don't think so.

Nothing hurts.

Me neither. You didn't win, though. Just so you know.

Then I said: What will Mom say? I think I meant it to be funny, a continuation of the joke, but the delivery was off and at the thought of her the tears came.

Everything is okay, you said, a little strangely, and because I felt like you were saying it for me, I agreed with you. We were seventeen and twenty-three. Then slowly we picked ourselves up, walked our bikes all the way back to the car. I don't know what moments like this have meant to you, but lately I've been carrying them around.

You never asked her what was going to happen next, like I did. In the end, what you allowed yourself wasn't a question but a command, and maybe that's the thing that actually brought her poisoned body back to life. One afternoon you said to her, I'm not going to lose another mother. Her eyes came into focus then. I believe she got better, in the end, for you.

WHAT WERE THE LONG-TERM EFFECTS of the early photo albums in the house, our mother's belly swollen with me, Grandma and Grandpa holding me as an infant, all the physical evidence of a history that contained the story of a life without you? Once I judged the amount of soy sauce you put on your rice and your face lit with fury.

Listen, Whitey, you said. I'm Thai, it's in my culture.

Whitey? I said.

How often did you consider our parents' features disclosed in mine? Our mother filled out the Family History form at the doctor's for you as long as she could.

Is there a history of the following in your family: heart disease, high blood pressure, thyroid disease, diabetes, cancer, depression, mental illness, stroke, lung problems, seizures, blood clots, kidney disease, bleeding problems.

N/A, N/A, N/A, she wrote.

Health problems in the immediate family: Father:___, Mother:___, Siblings:___. Sometimes she'd leave it blank and explain when she got inside. Though, arriving at the doctor's office with you, the questions usually answered themselves.

What were the long-term effects of our town, which, in spite of a national kidnapping case, prided itself on a kind of quaint safety? I saw our town differently after you came, though it was a difference I could still shed when I was alone. With you there were establishments to avoid, places that quieted when we walked in the door. There were parks where families stared in suspicion, churches, checkout lines, parking lots. Did they think we were kidnapping you if we picked you up too quickly? And the airport—how many times were we stopped at customs, asked for documents proving your name. With each subtlety I would look to you, brace for your fear and discomfort, the glances, the stares, the bad looks. I never said anything, hoping instead we could reroute around it, create some diversion to protect your feelings. You'd look back at me and shrug.

Once you asked our mother if she thought your birth mother was beautiful.

We don't know what the woman who gave birth to you in [Korea/India/Thailand] looked like, but because you are so [handsome/cute] we imagine that she must have been very beautiful. What do you think she looked like?

Of course, our mother said. Look at you.

―――――――

IT WAS A STRANGE TIME, the year leading up to your moving out. As our mother's health slowly recovered, electronics, including an unopened iPod, began to appear in your room again with brief explanations; our mother once again noticed you with items that she hadn't purchased. When you were accepted into a San Diego college, she wondered how you would do such a long drive away. But you felt certain you'd find at least a few people down there who looked like you, and you wanted to continue school, and when you framed it this way our father said that sending you off to college was a good thing. Everyone thought you were Hawaiian there, you reported back to me on the phone. You didn't correct them.

Midway through the year you called to tell me about a girl. You sent pictures: blond, blue-eyed. Under the spell of that romance, you used our father's credit card to purchase two first-class tickets home so she could meet the family. Our mother's voice went soprano again when she saw the credit card statement, our father's went baritone; the trip was canceled while our father spent two days on the phone trying to convince the airline to give him a refund. I don't think you realized that these costs weren't simple to shoulder, both our parents still working to pay a mortgage, the medical bills from our mother's cancer, retirement drifting farther away.

Sometimes I'd hang up with our mother and the rage would transport me to a dreamlike state. I'd bump into strangers on the walk to work, the image of you replaced by the sidewalk. Sometimes I would shake and shake your shoulders. Only I remembered the three of us cramped into our aunt's house when our father was out of work, I would tell your ghost, overhearing how they'd embellished their income on the adoption paperwork for fear that the real numbers would slow it down. I remembered the worry on our mother's face, the side jobs she picked up to pay our way through

Catholic school. Sometimes I actually called you and would yell a few of these things aloud, but in real life you never provided what I was probably looking for. *I'm sorry. I spend because x.* So I stopped calling when the next thing would happen, but I couldn't turn off that voice in my head, where I'd explain how the house, once incomplete in our waiting, now felt like something was missing again. I'd think of the weeks our father spent traveling, from city to city, from office to home, the time clocked at the desk, how the spending split the foundation he had worked hard to build. And I'd wonder again if this time I could forgive.

Why make this part of the story? I can hear you say. More honestly you'd say something like, *Why do you have to bring that up?*

Because suddenly it became a regular part of our life. Or had always been, somehow. Because the destruction increased with each cycle, only three of us left with visible remorse. They're on my case about money again, you'd tell me, and I'd ask how you'd twisted the sadness into this shape. Nobody wanted it three against one, but maybe it had already felt that way for so long that this frustration was what the money alleviated, if only temporarily. I didn't know then; I still don't. You were the only one, after all, with each restitution, reimbursement, restoration of our house, who couldn't hear the refrain of *I love you.* When I found out about the thousand dollars on unused plane tickets, I called and begged for a reason. The explanations made sense and they didn't. *I just wanted her to meet the family. It was the only available flight they had. I planned to pay it back later. I don't want to talk about this with you.*

ONE MORNING the house line rang; a stranger mentioned your name.

Why are you inquiring after my nineteen-year-old son? our mother said. Who is this? How did you get this number?

Loan sharks. You had debts to settle with two.
Honestly I don't remember how I spent it, you said.
Our father flew down to pay them off.

DON'T PAY it, I began telling our father. Don't fix it, don't enable it, don't help it. Don't help him. If he'd listened to me I don't know where you'd be. After the loans I took him to dinner and told him with conviction that it was the last time you should be saved. He looked at me in silence and I felt my face flush, realizing he still thought of me as a child. Now I wonder if he was actually just thinking that I wasn't a parent, that I didn't understand what to do with a sadness like that, the ongoing battle between instruction and protection, duty and anger, where responsibilities start and finally end. What should one do?

I THINK BACK now to your early visits home from college as if trying to track down missing evidence. Some nights, both of us back home for a weekend together, the four of us would sit around the table and you'd go the whole meal without saying a word. I would fill your silence with my own updates until finally someone would say, Danny? Anybody home?

Picture a house at night with all the lights on. See the woman at the table, awake with herself at odd hours. A voice carries in from the street, or a rustle in the bushes, or the scrape of a can kicked aside on the pavement or carried pitifully by the wind. Every time she looks out the window to question the darkness, all she can grasp is her own reflection.

Picture a house at night with all the lights on. Imagine a woman outside, staring in. No one can see her standing there, just on the other side of the pane, and at a certain point she just wants someone to turn out the lights so everyone can reclaim the privacy of the dark. She doesn't know if she's supposed to be standing there. It's her lawn, after all.

I want to ask you what you think I should do.

What should I do? Do I keep going?

Sometimes from my room I would hear the three of you downstairs, the latest bill that couldn't be paid, the odd purchase. Sometimes you had a job and sometimes you didn't. I would sit just outside of it and wonder how much I wanted to hear. Mostly I would hear all of you and long to leave, to forget you. I think I made a mistake in leaving so much unsaid between you and me. I was always waffling between ally or sellout, sister or mother, though you would be the first to say that the role of mother never fit me well. Because I wasn't your mother, not at all, and I never knew what to do. I should have asked you more about the money, about budgeting, about minimum payments, about what all that spending was trying to fill. I can see myself now in that house, contributing to the destruction, complicit in how much more we would face.

EVENTUALLY YOU MOVED to Reno, where you were accepted into a four-year university, with only a few semesters left. Our parents wanted more than anything to see you get your degree. When they went to visit you, you brought a new friend to lunch, who one day would become your best man.

I liked him from the moment I met him, though it was impossible not to notice how the two of you looked side by side: he stood about a foot above you, with curly red hair. He was so tall that his body would slump into a question mark around others, as if to ask if the distance bothered them. But your whole body seemed relaxed when you were with him. Your smile was different, your shoulders at ease; there were none of the edgy comments that usually signaled you were uncomfortable. When the two of you slept at my place one weekend, what I would remember is how after each meal your friend would thank me before standing up and washing the plates, just missing his head on all the doorways.

When he reached out to shake our father's hand that day, he leaned into you and whispered: Dude, your parents are white.

I know, you said.

YOU CAME HOME that first Christmas calling yourself a Christian. Our mother reminded you that you had been christened over twenty years ago, but you shook your head. It was suddenly very important for you to distinguish between your Catholic upbringing and your beliefs now.

You'd begun volunteering, attending church several times a week, and, most shockingly, reading the Bible, the only book I'd ever seen you willingly pick up. Sometimes you'd quote it to our mother in an argument; you'd post your favorite passages online. What's that, I said, when you changed your profile picture to a black bird, and you told me to look up Luke 12:24.

Consider the ravens: they neither sow nor reap, they have neither storehouse nor barn, and yet God feeds them. Of how much more value are you than the birds!

The change happened suddenly. But you talked openly about your newfound faith with our parents, as if to prove that it shouldn't worry them. You talked about it with our mother especially, who never missed a Sunday Mass. You and I didn't touch it; maybe because I'd long stopped going to church, or because we'd never spoken of God in all the years we'd sat next to each other in the pew. But it was strange to suddenly see the Holy Trinity on your Facebook wall, making regular visitations. That you could publish these thoughts on the internet but omit them from our phone calls sometimes made me feel far away from you.

How's everything with you?

Fine. You?

Fine.

But faith was just another item in a long list of things I no longer knew how to talk about. I could not explain the longing I felt every so often to believe in a system where pain carried larger, ethereal meaning. I just knew that I had asked for something and had not received it. I was angry that the sadness in the one life we'd been given could be explained away as sacrifice for the next.

But then again, I don't know if a thing like that can ever really leave you. It sits in your bones, whether you like it or not. Sometimes it made me want to crawl out of my skin and then, at the first sign of trouble, I could be filled with the deepest reverence for all of it, for the miracle of a body, for the humility of its failure, that it was loved and created so tenderly. If you'd asked me, I suppose I would have said that, even on my worst days, I saw prayer as a wide net of hopes and anxieties, released like a host of red and black balloons, trembling up, up, up. A letter was a kind of prayer, I hoped. A supplication to someone unseen. An adoration. A thanksgiving. A contrition. A love fused by the mysteries of joy and sorrow, like bound beads on a rosary. Maybe silence was a prayer, too.

BY FEBRUARY, it made more sense: there was a girl who also happened to be a Christian. During your spring break, you brought her home, via the white steed commonly known as your Honda, and one evening the two of you drove into the city for dinner.

I watched the girl with great curiosity as you both held hands on my couch. There had been many I'd come to know through our talks over the years, but this was the first to whom I'd been introduced. The girl wore no makeup, jean shorts, a sweatshirt, flip-flops. There was an innocence there that reminded me of you. And an intimacy was apparent between you; at many points in the conversation both of you would begin laughing and try, unsuccessfully, to explain the joke to my husband and me. We smiled politely, feeling not quite old, but stiff. Though I was pleased to see how funny she found you.

Did you consider me old, sitting opposite you, sipping white wine next to my husband? Crabby? Someone your girl would admire or fear? I couldn't tell. It was true that I had grown cynical over the years, and cautious when it came to you. But it was a relief to see you happy. And I realized, as you sat on the couch, arm around her, that you were the only person in my life who could make me feel time passing this way. Sitting there, you seemed so young to me, and still. There you were, drinking out of my wedding glasses, a little bit grown-up. There was the sense of wanting to slow things as the two of you walked out the door, thanked me for dinner, wished my husband and me good night.

ONLY ONCE during that time did you call and ask me for money, the only time, and I've thought about it ever since. Of course I know how interest works, you'd said. Your credit was destroyed at this point; you were waiting tables while in school and I was afraid to ask what the money was for. So I just told you no and we hung up angry. That night in bed I lay awake, wondering what I had done.

I READ SOMEWHERE that a baby remembers his mother's voice and face within thirty-six hours of birth. After only a few days in the world, he recognizes and prefers her native language, even when it's spoken by a stranger.

But a newborn doesn't recognize his father's voice, signaling that these preferences are formed in the symphony of the womb. The brain begins to decode and store his mother's language while he waits to meet her: her tone, her language patterns, so that he can be born into the world with memories of her.

L AST NIGHT at the rehearsal dinner I overheard someone ask when you knew that you had fallen in love, and I stopped the conversation I was in because I realized I didn't know the answer. Me? you said, in a kind of panic. You told the man who had asked that you didn't know.

Oh come on, the man said, a plus-one from the bride's side. What kind of answer is that on the day before your wedding?

THE VERY FIRST THING you'd told me about your bride was that she spent her early years in foster care. Your childhoods were marked by different cities, caretakers, classes, races, and yet there was something reflected there as each of you looked at the other. Neither of you spoke much about your birth parents, you said.

Much later you'd asked me: Could you see her as your sister?

It used to be easier to give you what you wanted. There used to be relief in its release, like a sigh, *Yes, take it*, your heart pinned there like a name tag, my name is blank and here's what I need. *My name is Danny and I need you to forget my mistakes. My name is Danny and here is my heart. My name is Danny and I need you to approve of my choices.* I'd said, I'll embrace whomever you marry as my sister, even though I knew it wasn't what you were looking for.

AFTER THE REHEARSAL DINNER I fell asleep early, but by midnight I was up again. I was realizing that I didn't know your love story at all, that I hadn't addressed it in the speech. And wasn't that the point? I just knew how you'd looked at her that evening at my apartment, your shoulders down, your smile big and relaxed. Maybe that was something any stranger could spot.

I got out of bed and went to the bathroom. Turned on the light, paged through the speech. I'd told my story, our story, the only story I knew. I remembered how our mother had said that from her bedroom, on the weekends you'd come to stay, she could hear you two laughing through the walls, an intimate laugh that wasn't meant to be put on display. Like two happy kids.

AT MY WEDDING our father said when I was growing up he could never envision the person I would marry. I would bring young men home and he would squint, hold out his fingers into two Ls, trying to fit them into some indistinguishable frame. And then one day a young man walked into his house, shook his hand in the kitchen, and suddenly a clearer picture came into focus. The mysterious alchemy of another's happiness. We change so much and so often that it's miraculous enough to keep pace with ourselves, let alone others.

Like our father, I had no clear vision for you. But then two things happened at once: you became very serious about the girl you were seeing, and you received the news that you'd been accepted on the mission trip you had mentioned at lunch, twelve countries in twelve months, Thailand in month two. You needed to raise ten thousand dollars for the trip.

I was skeptical when you told me this; I didn't understand the appeal in doing it this way and the money frightened me. I'd only imagined the version of this trip without the group, without the fundraising, where, selfishly, I came along, too. But our father had offered his encouragement, telling you he would help make the necessary arrangements to visit the Babies' Home if you wanted to see it. They had a website now, full of testimonials and smiling children, the pictures incongruous with my own memory. It was the first time that you'd ever spoken about returning to Thailand, our father reminded me, and if you wanted to raise the money and see the world beyond our own coast, who were we to stop you? Our father had traveled for work, I had traveled for work, and why shouldn't you have that, too? You had been better lately with your finances, our father said. You would do it the right way, our father said. You had a year to work and fundraise and save and you told our parents you knew you could do it. You wanted to go to the Babies' Home, to see where you ate and slept, so our father sent some emails. Soon our mother wore the idea more comfortably, too; she agreed that the trip would be good for you.

Then you called again with more news. I'll propose before I go, you said. What do you think?

I knew you weren't asking for honesty, but I ignored this. Aren't you a little young? I said. What's the rush?

I'm not young, you said quickly. And what difference does it make, anyway. You were young.

That was different, I said, and you laughed at me.

I've found the person I want to marry, you said. Can't you just be happy for me?

Afterward I called our parents and asked if it was productive to try to stop you. And did she understand your issues with money?

I think she understands him better than most, our mother said.

She's a good girl, our father said.

I suppose a lot can happen in a year apart, I said.

YOU CALLED BACK the next day to ask if I'd help you pick out a ring. I was surprised that you hadn't asked our mother, but this was an honor you'd bestowed upon me. So I drove home and picked you up and we stopped at three places on the east side of town.

No, no, no, you said, after each one I chose.

No, I said, when you examined the most expensive one in the case.

When you held the one you would buy, we became silent; I don't think we'd expected the moment to feel as tender as it did, both of us looking poorly slept under the fluorescent light. You smiled at me and it was a nice moment between us, the nicest in a while. I told myself that maybe all of this, the proposal, the trip, the money, maybe it would all turn out fine. You paid and the ring was placed in a black velvet box and then we started the car back toward home.

You snapped the box open and shut the whole ride, looking again every few minutes, as if to make sure it was still there. Just when you'd nodded with approval and closed it, I'd catch you re-examining it.

What's it like to be married? you asked me again.

WE HAD ALL PLANNED to spend a day at the beach and you decided this was the place to propose. Nervously we piled into the car, wound up Highway 1, and unloaded our coolers of snacks and drinks at a picnic table by the water. You threw around a Frisbee with your brother-in-law while the rest of us busied ourselves with blankets and chairs; our mother kept rearranging the crackers on the table until someone had to tell her to stop.

Finally you asked everyone if they wanted to take a walk. We nodded, feeling for the phones in our pockets. We began to make our way along the water like some ridiculous procession of ducks, the two of you up front with the rest of us tiptoeing behind. We walked so far and for so long that I began to wonder if you'd changed your mind, or if the bride had said something to give you cold feet. We turned around to whisper, tripping over one another's bare feet, our words lost to the wind. Then all of a sudden you stopped and turned to her, and we stopped, our breath stopped, maybe even time stopped just for us, while we watched you get down on one knee.

Some moments are as beautiful as you'd expect. What a thing it was to see you there, your future bride with one hand to you and the other to her mouth, covering a thousand-yard smile. Our father and my husband swarmed you like the paparazzi, while our mother and I held back and stared. Tears were running down our mother's cheeks, the wind pushing them sideways before they could fall straight down. When we came back to our picnic table our aunt had arrived and rounded up a few strangers from the beach to applaud your return. We toasted plastic cups of champagne with a host of warm, unfamiliar faces and wished you a long, happy life.

S HORTLY AFTER you came back from the mission trip, I moved from oral treatments to in vitro fertilization. I didn't speak to you or see you. In some ways this made the time before seem amateur, as if now, with this procedure, I had finally become professionally barren, a joke your brother-in-law did not find funny; he had stopped laughing at these kinds of jokes. I was very lucky, my doctor said, and it was true: my insurance extended to these treatments when most companies excluded it; without it, each extraction could cost anywhere from six to twenty thousand dollars. I am very lucky, I said. I went through several cycles that involved new bills, new injections, new diets, anesthesia, and no drinking in a time when part of me longed for a beer more deeply than for a child. This is the part that began to haunt me: that the pain had blurred the desire. Do I still want this? I said only to myself, too ashamed to tell our mother, your brother-in-law, the newest secret I'd taken to carrying around. It seemed cruel at this point to be working so hard when there were already so many liv- ing, breathing, existing children in need of a parent, children I'd seen for myself. How did we get here? New decisions linked only to previous ones, wherever we last left off, route D if not route C if not route B, rather than to the longings of my body, my heart, which had become unknown to me. Not viable, the doctor said after the first cycle, then again for the second and the third. I know they're in there, I told the doctor, conspiratorial; I'd seen them myself, spoken to them on the long walks home. The ones we've taken are not viable, he repeated, as if speaking to someone who needed things repeated.

IF THERE WAS ONE THING our mother hated more than anything, it was people telling her what a good thing she'd done. She was often answering to correlations between you and some kind of civic duty. How many people through the years lauded her for her service, how often she felt the tap on her shoulder at checkout, as if she'd spent a year in a war overseas rather than fighting the day-to-day battles of having a family at home.

What are they talking about? you'd say to her, sometimes loudly enough that the person could hear it, and only then would it occur to them that they'd said something strange, and they'd turn back to their cart with a shame that seemed to confuse them.

Sometimes people had the wrong ideas about adoption, our mother would go over again in the car. Sometimes it was hard for people to understand if they hadn't experienced it themselves. About why people did things.

People never say the right thing about anything, you said once, after one of these episodes, and I remember looking at you from the front seat, because it was clearly an unshakable truth, and one I would return to as an adult.

Then our mother would say: You are my son because I wanted to be your mother. So if anything, I was terribly selfish.

Everyone should tell you you're terrible instead, you would say, and she would say, Yes, probably they should, and the two of you would smile.

At the library one afternoon I found an extract from *The Literary Digest*'s April 8, 1916, issue, which quoted a Mrs. Charles F. Judson, maybe one of the first to figure out how to gratify white, infertile, middle-class women. She privately placed children out of her home in Philadelphia and had three hopes for her work:

> *First.*—To make happy many empty and discontented homes, and thus, perhaps, to diminish the divorce-evil . . . So many people are bored with life who do not realize they are not leading a normal family life, since no family can be complete or normal without children and the happiness they bring.
>
> *Secondly.*—To give the little ones a chance in life . . . Unless the spiritual part of a child is cared for, it may become a menace to the community, whereas with culture and training, it will become a joy.
>
> *Thirdly.*—To give our country more of the best class of American citizens. Our forebears, through toil and struggle, often gained ideals, culture, refinement, and beliefs which have built up this nation . . . If a child is adopted and these ideas and beliefs passed down to it, we create another American citizen, guided by the same uplifting faiths as held and helped our forefathers.

Was it Angelina Jolie who did this to us? you would joke when you got older. Mia Farrow? Madonna? We'd come to acknowledge ourselves as a math problem in the face of strangers, but we couldn't figure out who had made the look of us charitable. Singer and dancer Josephine Baker was one of the first celebrities to make a public statement about transracial families in the fifties, referring to her adoptive household of twelve as the "rainbow tribe," raising children from Korea, Japan, Finland, Colombia, North Africa, France, Venezuela, Morocco, and the Ivory Coast. On days when the family was at home in the Château des Milandes, tours were arranged so visitors could walk the grounds and witness how natural they'd find the scene.

As the aughts arrived, as our mother watched the life we'd been leading transform into celebrity trend, she looked away from stories that spoke of fame and money expediting the process. Five years, she told those who asked.

Even all those years later, when you were an adult, when the pictures left the magazines, when every set of famed parents had divorced, the words still flew back to her, like an old, loyal paper plane. A tap on her shoulder. What a wonderful thing you've done, they'd say.

And what have you inherited as an American?

ON OUR WORST DAYS with you growing up, our mother would say, I should never have taken him out of his country. She often worried that she had done you a disservice by bringing you here. She worried that it hadn't been a wonderful thing at all.

Other days she would say: But he's had a good life.

The poet Mary-Kim Arnold writes: *As a Korean child growing up in a white family, in a white neighborhood, what I was aware of most was being conspicuous. Rarely did I go unnoticed. Unquestioned. But being visible is not the same as being seen.*

Mrs. Charles Judson says: *He shall have had a hand in the building of the nation and of the world.*

Our mother wondered: Was love enough?

THE MORNING of your wedding I head down the hall to our mother's room, where I find her pacing in the thin hotel robe that hangs in all of the closets. She tells me our father's out pacing the grounds.

We have an hour before we meet the bride in her room, so I direct our mother to the bathroom mirror, where she begins winding the hot rollers into her hair, the ones she's taken on every trip with her since the eighties. We replay the events from the previous evening at the rehearsal, the strangers who are cast to star together in a wedding. I tell her about the romance that seems to have sprung up between a groomsman and one of the bride's cousins; I do not tell her about the guest who plucked a bottle from behind the bar before leaving, wedging it unsuccessfully in her purse.

How are you feeling? I'd asked you as the guests started to leave, and your bride answered for you.

You were nervous, she said, you didn't like the attention. You offered a shrug as some sort of agreement.

I see, I said, and then felt a funny thing well up in me, as if I were supposed to acknowledge to your bride that she knew you better than I did.

I take a seat on the bathroom floor and look up at our mother as she applies her eyeshadow. Our hearts are preoccupied with simpler questions: who will drive the car, who will bring the rings, who will remember to take the flower girl's petals out of the fridge. I read our mother the speech, and she interrupts to remind me to thank the bride's side at the beginning, all the cousins and aunts and friends who have traveled. She writes *THANK U BRIDE* at the top of the page so I won't forget, and I wonder if we're all collectively feeling that in some way today. THANK U BRIDE for loving our son, our brother. THANK U BRIDE for promising to take care of him. I ask her if she thinks you'll be happy with what I've written. Then our father comes in with three coffees and we sit there in the bathroom for a few minutes, drinking in the last few quiet moments of the day.

WHAT DO YOU THINK, you'd said, stepping out of the dressing room. Your brother-in-law and I were waiting on the couches of the Men's Wearhouse, fearing the fate of our own outfits. We were six months out from the wedding by then, and this was only the second time I'd seen you since you'd come back from the mission trip.

Purple, your brother-in-law whispered, as you pulled back the curtain to reveal your suit.

You look like an eggplant, I said.

You frowned and studied the tag. It says "indigo gray," you said, and looked at yourself again in the mirror. I think I look nice.

What if the groomsmen don't wear the jackets? you conceded, after a moment. Just the pants and the matching vests?

Have you ever seen the California Raisins? I said, and your brother-in-law squeezed my knee. It's your outfit, too, I whispered, examining the price tag, relieved that if anything it would at least be a rental.

Never heard of them, you said, keeping your eyes on the mirror. Somehow your bride was nowhere to be found, though I'm sure she would have only stuck up for you. I think it looks nice, you said again, and your reflection smiled.

Blue is also very nice on you, I said a little curtly.

Dark blue, your brother-in-law said.

You shrugged. Well, you two are older, anyway, you said.

So? I said.

Maybe when you have kids you'll be more in touch, you said. You know, understand what's good with the younger generation?

Then you looked at my face and frowned. What? you said. What did I say?

ABOUT A YEAR AGO, I went to visit a close friend who'd just had a baby. The scene in her apartment was harrowing: burp cloths and baby loungers and nipple pads lay like debris from a recent explosion. I'd heard that newborns slept a lot, but this one cried the entire visit, the noise prehistoric. I stared into its little red face, a lump of clay fixed into unhappiness, and tried to think of an honest compliment. Good strong lungs! I said.

The doctor said he would settle down in just a few more months, my friend explained loudly. I'd been there five minutes and the promise felt like a death sentence. I went home and opened a forbidden bottle of wine and drank it very quickly.

Recently, I went back to visit that friend. Her apartment was still a mess when I walked in, but I was shocked to find the creature gone; a little boy took his place on the couch.

He smiles with his whole face, I said, and this time I was a little in awe of him.

Ten months, she said, as the baby clutched the hair on her neck. And as I looked at that boy who was so in love with his mother, I realized I was thinking of you. He knew exactly who she was, this boy, who was about the same age as you when your life changed. Of course you had known who she was then, even if you couldn't remember it now. That recognition was all I could see.

ZOOLOGIST KONRAD LORENZ studied this recognition while observing goslings following their mother through the wild. Immediately after hatching, he said, the birds' neural system was programmed to attach to the first object they saw, *imprinting*, he called it, when young locked on to a mother's characteristics. But it was later proved that this system can be fooled—studies showed lambs forming attachments to televisions, guinea pigs to wooden blocks, monkeys to cloth bundled into the rough outline of a simian mother. It wasn't the most romantic argument for adoptive bonding, but wasn't it an argument, nonetheless? That primal love could be reprogrammed, redirected?

YOU SHOULD CALL HIM, your brother-in-law said after the incident with the suit. Talk to him about what's been going on with us.
    Stay out of it, I said.

IN THE THIRTEENTH CENTURY, Holy Roman emperor Frederick II tried to determine the inborn language of mankind by raising a group of children without speech. Foster mothers and nurses were instructed to suckle, bathe, and wash the group of test children, but not to speak to them under any circumstances, so the emperor could witness whether the first words out of their mouths would be Hebrew, Greek, Latin, or Arabic. But in the absence of sound, all the infants died before yielding any kind of linguistic result.

Centuries later, in the 1940s, psychoanalyst René Spitz described orphaned children raised in institutions who were fed and clothed, kept warm and clean, but were not played with or held to protect against exposure to infectious organisms. Spitz found that while the physical needs of the children were met, they soon became ill, withdrawn, and underweight. And in a strange twist, the infants became exceedingly vulnerable to the measles.

Spitz ended up publishing his findings with this central argument: For a child, love is necessary for survival. Could there really be a home without someone who welcomes you there?

But what about the more pressing question: Did it matter who that someone was?

LOVE ISN'T BOUND UP in food, said psychiatrist John Bowlby, the creator of attachment theory. He disagreed with Freud, who believed a baby's first relationship with his mother focused mostly on her breast. Love is primary, Bowlby said, attachment is primary; we're not conditioned to love merely because someone feeds us. We love certain people and we need them to love us back. His studies showed that as children became toddlers, this need only intensified. They grieved when their mother left them, they understood a loss. They wanted their mothers back.

I ONLY KNOW ONE COUPLE my age that has adopted, a close friend and his husband. Maybe I should call him, I say to your brother-in-law, get a clearer picture of what it might look like.

You need a clearer picture? he says.

I don't tell him that one afternoon in Safeway I see a little girl in a shopping cart, two or three years old, with hair that springs wildly in all directions, and I feel such a wave of fresh longing that

I actually need to hold on to something, and clutch at the handle on a frozen food door. Maybe I could do it, I think, as she and her mother wheel past me. I could run away from all this, the doctors, these treatments; I could love and care for a child that didn't come from me. I could make my body just a body again, rather than some kind of lonely spaceship, trawling the darkest spaces for new life.

YOU'RE THE ONLY BABY that I've ever found comfort with, still a baby to me, even though you were three years old. Picking you up was like breathing. I'd never had that before, growing up in the company of adults, and it was such a relief to finally understand the physical closeness of a sibling. It's surprised me that this comfort has never transferred over to the children I've held as an adult, only magnifying the hollowness of my own body, how singular I am in its frame. I've mourned the missing comfort, that the mother across from me knows something I don't. I've mourned that we never had you as an infant.

The image I keep coming back to is the apple tree that stood next to the deck in the backyard. Every year it would overproduce and you and I would compete daily with the birds, scrambling to eat as many apples as we could. Womanhood, as I used to see it, was that tree in full bloom, the fruit protruding from the leaves like a blush. Motherhood was the afternoons we spent pulling as much as we could from those branches, smacking away with the deep, simple pleasure of children. And what I've felt lately is akin to the afternoons I sat alone on the deck, listening to each apple fall to the ground, wasting its sweetness.

———

WHAT'S IT LIKE TO BE MARRIED, you'd asked me. To be married is to know the way he sits in his chair when he's concentrating. His back hunches and his feet tuck under, as if his whole body is tightening to keep grasp on an idea. The sounds he makes in his sleep, how he'll order off a menu, that he'd choke and die before sending anything back.

I'd say that to be married is to make peace with all you cannot see, as hard as you try. For instance, the gray space of his life before me, before our life in California, growing up on the other side of the country, raised in a city apartment with one brother and one sister. When we began dating and I asked him to tell me stories about his childhood, about three children on top of one another in a city apartment, he'd say that he didn't really remember. At first I didn't believe this, attributing the lack of detail to something unhappy, but soon I realized he was telling the truth. The few memories he keeps are often told out of order, his features strained, like a person who's been tasked with describing the qualities of the air, or the taste of water. Sometimes I find myself correcting him based on some earlier version I've heard from his mother or sister. That's probably it, he'll say, nodding. He doesn't seem obligated to the past, and this is what keeps him mostly mysterious to me, as if he could have been anyone before, as if anything could have happened, as if the old stories could still change, and he might recount them one day when we are old, with a shrug. His days as a pirate or a pimp, a king. I don't know if mystery is the thing that holds people in love, though, or the way one sits in a chair. I don't know if it's the absence of familiar pain in a person, or the recognition of one.

To be married is to live with both things at once, the knowing and the mystery. One evening not too long ago, I had a heart monitor strapped to my chest, as prescribed by the doctor. I wasn't allowed to shower but was embarrassed to go into work in the morning with the slick sheen of my hair. Your brother-in-law put a towel on the floor, filled up our pitcher, made sure the water wasn't too hot or too cold. At thirty-something years old we leaned back against the floor as he washed my hair in the tub, the heart monitor protected under a sweatshirt. He leaned over with a look so concentrated I began laughing, a girlish laugh, because I'd known him and lived with him for years and never once had we crossed into this territory, stretching tremulously into the future, picturing ourselves old and sick, before hurrying back into our young bodies. And again I realized I had been crazy to think that marriage was not for me. He leaned over to pat my hair dry and I thought, thank God sometimes we are wrong about things.

FORTY MINUTES A DAY I ride one of the most expensive and problematic light rails in the country, spend time under the San Francisco Bay with a slice of the 400,000 people who must also succumb to this obstinate beast. While riding, I have watched people sleep, open to every kind of vulnerability. I have watched men and women apply their makeup, clip their nails; one night a gentleman gave himself a haircut in the seats reserved for the elderly. I have watched people watch porn, watched arguments, watched acquaintances try to keep conversation, witnessed crying; I have cried myself. Once a packed train got stuck underground and as the claustrophobia caved in I felt a hand on the back of my shirt, as if trying to pull me out of myself. I was embarrassed, mostly, that the shirt was soaked from the fear of being trapped down there, waiting for daylight forever. May I? an older woman said softly and I nodded even though I didn't know what she was asking for. And suddenly she was rubbing my back, the circles slow and rhythmic, the comfort shocking, the woman whispering: There, there, almost there.

How to feel so close to her in that moment, and yet so desperately far from you?

DON'T YOU EVER GET SAD? you'd asked me.

Every Tuesday at noon I get sad, when an alarm goes off in the city, a fifteen-second wail followed by a voice that says, *This is a test. This is a test of the Outdoor Public Warning System. This is only a test.* The entire office can hear it from our desks, and sometimes I watch the new hires, their eyes shifting to the rest of us to gauge the danger.

During World War II, fifty sirens were mounted across the city to warn of air raids and have been going off every Tuesday ever since. Today there are 109 perched on the poles and buildings of San Francisco, Treasure Island, and Yerba Buena, ten of which are solar-powered. The siren call has its own Twitter feed and nineteen decent reviews on Yelp (average four out of five stars, only open on Tuesdays). I've been at this job for five years now, next to siren 92, which means in the last five years I've felt sad at least 260 times.

I AM WAITING, and everything around my waiting is stricken with unreality, Barthes writes. *In this café, I look at the others who come in, chat, joke, read calmly: they are not waiting.*

WHEN DO YOU THINK you'll have kids? you'd asked not long after I had started the treatments, unaware of the drama backstage, that your sister was trying and failing already. I don't remember how I answered.

What do you think it's like to be a mom? you'd said.

I had some clues, like the cards our mother used to send when

I moved far away. *I love you!* sometimes was all it said, in her cursive. I kept them in a box under my bed, where I imagined each one glittering in the dark.

I always had the feeling growing up that life before children was like some kind of cloud you couldn't see through, some kind of city obscured by the morning fog. On the other side, I imagined, the sun was outrageously bright, warming or burning your chest, shoulders, hands, depending on the day.

AM I IN LOVE? writes Barthes. *Yes, since I'm waiting.*

TODAY EVEN STRANGERS CAN SEE that your bride is happy. She's wound her hair back into a sophisticated knot with two dark pearls pinned in her ears. It's the first time I've seen her in lipstick and the deep shade illuminates the rest of her face, almost as if theater lights have been held up to it at all angles. Young beauty, I'm reminded, is always so shocking. When our mother and I knock on her door this afternoon, she greets us with a smile but I can see that she's frightened. Come in, she says, and we walk into her hotel room, where a few of her bridesmaids sit quietly on the bed. How about a little music? I say, and she nods, pulling me aside. I'm not nervous to marry your brother, she says, just so you know. I'm nervous for all the pictures. Just wait until you put on the dress, I say. Our mother and I sit with the other girls, snipping tags and tearing price stickers off shoes, while your bride gets her hair and makeup done. Then finally, after an hour or so, we bring the dress over. Our mother helps her with the lacing at the back and only then does the reality of the day present itself in the mirror, and your bride can see that she has never been more exquisite.

It's good, right? she says.

It's perfect, our mother says.

OUR MOTHER collects the bride's train and we process along the corridor, the additional bridesmaids following. The girls' faces are as soft as the petals gathered in the basket, waiting to be tossed out to the wind. The bride has chosen a beautiful pale blue for the dresses, and I see only a cast of young Virgin Marys in front of me. I lean in and whisper to our mother that I am the only bridesmaid old enough to have birthed the entire wedding party and she says very seriously, That's mathematically untrue. We stop downstairs at the hotel entrance, where Noreen waits, our site coordinator for the day, who runs around with a clipboard and headset as if she is directing the Rockettes. She waits for the cue and then opens the doors, and we make our way down to the beach, not far from the spot where you proposed.

Ahead of us are fifty white chairs, twenty-five to each side, with ranunculus and baby's breath strung along the aisles. The sand seems to glow in the five-o'clock light. We have most of the beach to ourselves, except for the stranger fifty yards away who's photographing the scene with an iPad. My dress tucks under my feet in the sand and I suddenly become so fixated on not tripping up the aisle that I forget to look at you. How do I forget to look at you? I take my place to the left and peer over the other bridesmaids' heads and from the side I can see you in your suit, next to your brother-in-law and your best man, who ended up making it to the wedding, after all. I look out and see our aunt and the familiar faces of friends and cousins. You're giving the crowd your toothy smile reserved for school photos, a nervous smile. How did I forget to look at you as I walked up?

Then the music changes and your bride is here and the teeth are gone from your smile. You look at her with reverence, like fireworks coming up over the hill, just for you.

OUR PARENTS never got to see you walk down the aisle when you finished college because you forgot to fill out the commencement form. This, after you'd ordered the cap and gown, after our parents had the hotel reserved, the restaurant where they would take you out to dinner. You'd called to tell our mother the day before, as she was packing the banner she'd made, the words screaming from the inside of her luggage CONGRATULATIONS GRADUATE! They canceled the trip and you promised to mail them the diploma.

It ended up being one of those moments, though, your rare ability to turn it all around, to still make them so happy. You drove home a week later and told me to meet you there; we stacked a few chairs in the backyard and hooked up your phone to a portable speaker. It was a ninety-five-degree day in Petaluma but you ran upstairs and put on your gown and cap and when you called our mother outside I turned on YouTube's most popular rendition of "Pomp and Circumstance." And down you processed through the lawn chairs in your gown, and our mother snapped a picture as I handed you the Saturday edition of *The Press Democrat*, since your diploma wasn't set to arrive for another six weeks. Our father took the chair next to our mother and they clapped while you accepted the paper, threw your cap up to the sky.

THE DAY after I got engaged you called and asked if you'd have to make a speech. I'd forgotten this until recently, how you'd asked about the speech before offering your congratulations. I pushed the question away, cranky about being asked anything yet, telling you instead not to worry, that you weren't on the hook if you didn't want to be.

When the day came almost two years later, my husband's sister spoke, my husband's brother spoke, then our father and my best friend spoke for me. I could tell when you came up to me later that you regretted not volunteering, or resented that I hadn't pushed, that the speech signaled something important and to be excluded had not provided relief but the certainty that you'd been cut. I had told you it was really no big deal, that I hadn't wanted to overwhelm you, but I'll admit now that I didn't push because I wasn't sure what you were going to say. What would you write about me?

Instead I'd asked you to sign as witness on my marriage certificate and you practiced your name three times on scratch paper first: Danny Larsen, Danny Larsen, Danny Larsen, still hardly legible on the final document, the letters small and unruly.

I'm sorry now that I didn't ask you to speak at my wedding, that I was too caught up in the guest list, the dress, the food, the kind of person I swore I'd never be. In the months leading up to your wedding, all the same details passed between me and your bride.

Had I had a guest book? she said. Had I had a cake? He'll just want whatever you had, you know.

AREN'T YOU JEALOUS you can't have a tan like me? you'd said once, when we were on vacation. You held your arm against mine and we examined my ugly blue veins, interstates across my wrist. You smiled, pleased with yourself.

What's it like to be grown up? you'd asked, but we were still kids then, and thankfully I didn't have to answer.

You never asked me if I thought your birth mother was beautiful. This was a question reserved only for our mother.

I used to write about your birth family sometimes when I was younger. They were strange little stories that always filled me with shame. One started with your sister ringing the doorbell looking for you, pushing past me into the house, leaving her fingerprints all over the photographs.

Do they stand there with us today, as palpable as the fog, as a flock of birds netted over the sky? The sun sits complacent while the wind battles the dresses and hair spray, the ribbons attached to the seats. The locals nestle into their chairs with coats and sunglasses and the visitors wonder what kind of summer beach wedding this is. But they can't say the scene isn't beautiful: the water is tinsel on the horizon, and closer in, just framing the bride and groom, it's a deep, restless blue.

Why don't you call me more often? you'd asked.

But the bottom of our feet match, you'd told me once, long, long ago. You whispered it in my ear like an old secret between us.

I miss you, you'd said.

A MAN WALKS DOWN THE BEACH while the officiant winds his way through Corinthians: *Love is patient, love is kind . . . For God is not a God of disorder but of peace.* The man is holding a metal detector, following it obediently along the shore. I've left my glasses off for the pictures and squint hard to get a better look. As he approaches I realize that it's not a metal detector but only a small dog on a leash, but the mix-up dizzies the moment, like a dream, like the poorest of comparisons.

This morning, hours before the ceremony began, you called our mother and asked what exactly a vow was. You came to our mother's room and when I knocked on the door with pastries I found the two of you on the hotel love seat, hunched over a legal pad. Can I help with anything? I asked, and you'd said, prideful, No. So I shut the door and went downstairs where I found our father sitting alone at one of the breakfast tables. I took a seat across from him and he said good morning and then we gave each other a long look.

WHEN YOU WERE ACCEPTED on that mission trip, twelve countries in twelve months, our father was the first to tell you to go.

You needed to raise all that money, and somewhere along the way you'd left the job in Reno, so you took a position at one of the vineyards north of Petaluma, working for their website. You moved back in with our parents to help save and wrote an appeal to every family member and friend to donate to the trip. You'd never left the country, and now you'd be returning to Thailand for the first time on your own, you'd be visiting some of the poorest corners of the world to build houses and take part in other charitable activities. I offered to help you with the letter, but you declined, and the three of us never saw what you sent. Apparently what you had written was effective, though: soon there were more people invested in the hope that the return would fulfill something, change something, and even those who didn't have much to give contributed, believing in the greater cause, which was actually not the poorest corners of the world but you. Eventually our parents offered to match what you raised, and then there was an entire community of people who felt like they were some small part of sending you on your way. Perhaps we'd aligned ourselves with those notions of charity after all, with those who thanked us for our service for so many years.

All of this had started as a way to support your return, and as it built on itself I kept trying to see it as our parents did, because if you were curious to see where you came from, how could they not help you get there?

Maybe they thought it would set you up better for life, for relationships, for interviews, for work, because with each passing year there was a larger question about how you would fare in the world on your own. At some hazy point in the timeline, things seemed dicey with your future bride and we all feared the trip would be canceled. She was still living in Reno and driving to our parents' house on the weekends to see you. But you insisted you would still be going without her, you would do long distance; the proposal happened just weeks before you left.

The night before your departure, I threw you a goodbye party at my apartment with our parents, our aunt, your best man, and a few others who had given to the trip. After work, I rushed to the store for a cake that read *Happy Travels!* and we all ate it anxiously while you and your future bride held hands under the table.

I'm proud of you, I said, but I couldn't tell if you were too nervous to hear it.

The rest of the group was proud that evening, too. We ended up going around the table, telling stories about you. We talked about meeting you that first day in the orphanage, the white bear, the puke in the car. We talked about that long, long plane ride home, about Disneyland, about that time an opossum got in the house. You sat there quietly and listened, and at the time I thought you were happy to hear it. It seemed to me that all your life you had wanted a moment like this: filled with recognition, purpose, ambition, and most of all, our approval for you to go on your way. Though now I think I'm wrong about this, that I've had no idea what exactly you've wanted all your life. What have you wanted?

Did you know then that you weren't going to make it to the end of the first month, let alone the year? You stayed for three weeks before purchasing a ticket back to Reno, just a few days before the group made it to Thailand. You used your remaining funds to put down a deposit on a new apartment with your future bride.

I don't want to talk about it.

But why?

I don't want to talk about it.

But why did you leave?

I just wanted to come home.

But the money? What's going to happen to the money?

I said I don't want to talk about it with you.

It was our father who drove to see you a few months later, to help you once you began the old spending habits there, to process what you'd done, or hadn't. Because this was how you'd taught yourself to cope, and soon the credit card companies deactivated your accounts, the rest of your money disappeared, and in its place came an eviction notice for your apartment. Once again the debt began to pile.

When you opened the door, our father walked into the room you could no longer afford, examined the items collecting dust. He helped you pack your things and find a new place to live with your fiancée, who could no longer shoulder the cost of both of you. He paid off the credit cards, the security deposit for the new apartment, the neglected payments toward your car. He and our mother were on the cusp of retirement. And all that time, our mother and I never knew exactly what words were exchanged between you and our father, only that he stayed for many days, he stayed until, once again, it was all cleaned up. We assumed that there were more promises made, words our father knew well by then. And the spending might have been forgivable in time, as it always was, chalked up to the cyclical nature of addiction, of the tornado of need and confusion collecting more and more in its path, except then, after all that kindness, you took again.

ARISTOTLE LIVED with a guardian, and Augustus, the first emperor of the Roman Empire, was an adopted heir to the throne. Andal, a

Tamil saint, was found in a temple garden, and raised by the man who found her. Batman was orphaned, Robin was orphaned and adopted by Batman. Spider-Man was raised by his aunt and uncle, Tarzan by apes in the jungle. Boba Fett found refuge with a bounty hunter, Snow White with a cottage of dwarves, Curious George with his captor in the yellow hat. James Bond went to live with his aunt, Superman was adopted by farmers. Beowulf was raised by his grandfather before becoming the king of the Geats. Oedipus was abandoned on a mountain and rescued by a shepherd.

Romulus and Remus were nursed and cared for by a wolf. Edgar Allan Poe was taken in by a foster family at age two, Bertrand Russell by grandparents at three, Ivan IV by feuding boyar families at eight, Herbert Hoover and Leo Tolstoy by relatives at nine, Eleanor Roosevelt and W. Somerset Maugham by relatives at ten, Joseph Conrad by an uncle at eleven, J. R. R. Tolkien by a Catholic priest at age twelve. Moses was raised as an Egyptian, Muhammad was sent to live with a Bedouin family in the desert.

Jean-Jacques Rousseau and Cato the Younger were raised by their uncles. Edward Albee was adopted as an infant, John Keats was raised partly by his grandmother.

Malcolm X lived in a series of foster homes, Nelson Mandela was placed under the guardianship of a Tembu regent.

Friedrich Nietzsche and René Descartes and Isaac Newton were all cared for by grandmothers; Elizabeth I was taken in by a baron who would later try to take her as his wife.

Little Orphan Annie was adopted by a billionaire businessman, Alexander Hamilton by a wealthy merchant, Paddington Bear by the family who found him at a train station.

It still surprises me when I hear people call us different. It shouldn't, I suppose, but it does. I want to tell them that unconventional families have been here, in the literature, the mythology, the history, the religion. Convention is just a failure to see it.

ABOUT A WEEK BEFORE the wedding, I spend a Saturday reading a book at the library. I stay until the tables are empty and a woman asks me to pack up my things. The book is nonfiction, about an American Arctic explorer who brings a group of Inuit from Greenland to New York City in the late 1800s, delivering them as a living exhibition to the American Museum of Natural History. The group is promised passage home in a year, but they are not told that they'll be housed in the museum's basement, where the superintendent allows select visitors to come and inspect them. Large crowds begin to peer through a grating where they can look down on the group in their quarters.

When most of the Inuit die of pneumonia shortly afterward, one of the children in the group is adopted by the superintendent and his wife. The boy grows close with his adoptive mother and continues to spend time at the museum's Eskimo exhibit, surrounded by the material brought south by the explorer. The boy doesn't realize until several years later that his father's bones have been exhibited there in the museum, too, right in front of him, that they'd been preserved and displayed after his death in New York.

The boy makes a case for his father's bones to be returned to Greenland, but this isn't granted in his lifetime. Instead he eventually travels home, relearning his native tongue and way of life. He returns to the States a few years before his death and is buried in Pittsburg, New Hampshire.

When I step out of the library I remember that the day was warm when I got there, but now wind abuses the streets. I walk toward the Ferry Building, past restaurants and bars and boarded-up windows. And I want more than anything in that moment to ask you if the past should just be left to rest, if that's the way you'd prefer it. Because I can't tell anymore if digging it up is an act of love, or if it's stringing up your insides in a window. I can't tell if all of this is an exhumation for which you have or have not granted permission.

WHEN OUR FATHER RETURNED HOME the credit card company flagged fraudulent activity, then canceled his cards due to the enormity of the charges, and of course he wondered but then put the thought aside, wondered but then put the thought aside; you were no longer on his card, he reminded himself. He wouldn't have guessed that you'd written down his number and security code during his visit, charged more concerts and clothing and equipment while he sat in the next room handling your bills, that you would sell the items for cash as soon as he left, as if the name on the card didn't connect to the man you loved, as if pocketing the cash would mean you wouldn't have to ask for more help. When the company called back to tell our father the zip code where the purchases had been made he said nothing at first to the women, instead wandering alone in his own house, perhaps introducing the thought to each room he passed: This is the den where my son has taken from me, this is the kitchen where he has lied, this is the bedroom where I must acknowledge his addiction, the garage where I've chosen to keep my pain to myself, unsure how to explain it to my wife, my daughter, the world.

Will you take this man? the officiant asks.

The months passed and a silence grew between us again. I spent the weekends at home, unsure how to face the hours unoccupied by work. It had become bigger than the three of us this time, the destruction let out of the house. *I've lost you, I've lost you*, said my footsteps, my heart. I had lost you, the damage irreparable. But of course it was the opposite. Because really you had lost me. I continued to visit our parents, often returning without your brother-in-law, slowly reverting back to the old unit, and eventually the anger was replaced with a sadness. *Never threaten abandonment*, the books said. *You cannot take away your child's pain.* You reconciled with our parents after a few months, but a year stretched on without a word between us.

Then, the sound of your voice. That first phone call. It was almost Christmas. Like hearing from the dead in a dream. Hello, hello? my chest saying. Brother, is that you? Then the frost. Brother, brother, what do you want. You can't find it here. You were working a lot, you said. You still planned to get married. I said things had been hard for our parents, and you said that things had been hard for you, too. You asked how I was and for some reason all I could think to answer was *dead*. I have been the walking dead, thanks, and you? Then we hung up angry and I didn't know what would happen next.

THE OFFICIANT asks if you will take this woman, and I wonder if a person can take love without forgiveness. You agree to love her in sickness and in health, but just how far does sickness extend? No one ever asks about agreeing to love in the absence of self-correction.

THREE AREAS OF THE BRAIN affect monetary decisions. The amygdala responds to winning and losing; the prefrontal cortex organizes learning associations from past successes and mistakes; and the anterior cingulate cortex helps judge the value of a reward. It's the anterior cingulate cortex that activates that awful feeling in the pit of your stomach when an anticipated reward fails to show up. Or, money issues can all simply come down to dopamine neurons, which, when fired, create the euphoric feeling associated with risk.

Instead of picking up the phone in the months after the mission trip, I read about a gambling test conducted on people with complications in their prefrontal cortices or amygdalae. Subjects are given four decks of cards. In decks A and B, the possible immediate reward is high, but the decks also include cards that have a high penalty. In decks C and D the reward is low, but in choosing consistently from those decks the subject will experience an overall gain. The experiment showed that problems in the amygdala prevented the triggering of discomfort toward the riskier decks. Problems in the prefrontal cortex showed an inability to transfer information from past experiences, resulting in the continuous selection of high-penalty cards. When these issues were present, players could not make advantageous choices, even though they were able to think about what they were doing.

THE THIEF *is not looking for the object that he takes*, the pediatrician and psychoanalyst D. W. Winnicott writes, and I think, not the thief, the child. *He is looking for a person. He is looking for his own mother, only he does not know this.*

GIVEN THE CHANCE, there is so much I would have done differently. And somewhere, in the quiet place where you process things, I know there is remorse.

I just no longer know what I need to believe in: that you can see the consequences, or that you can't.

L OOK AT ANY ADOPTION PLOT and you'll see the same picture: a stranger steps into the house to build it up or burn it all down. The absence of history, or the inability to rewrite it, keeps tensions high, that handful of blank years you can never take back. I'd never noticed the role the house itself can play. Destruction is transitive, after all, requiring an object on which to act.

Where is the third option, of a house caught in an endless cycle? Composition, demolition, composition, demolition, composition, demolition.

IF THE VICTORIANS COULD OFFER one resolution, it would be true love. A marriage that might look beyond it all, to reset the cycle. Though what happens next they never seem to say.

WEDDINGS DO STRANGE THINGS to people. Recently at a wedding in Montana I slipped out of the tent and ran half a mile into the surrounding wilderness. I didn't stop until I felt alone enough to scream, a scream similar to the one you used to make as a child, part moan, part howl at the moon, the pain bright and unsure of itself, laboring itself out. I will never be able to identify all the feelings that were bound up in that sound of yours, but I can name mine: by then I had been trying for four years to have a child, and as I stood there, heels sunk into the field, I didn't know how much longer I'd be willing to wait.

I asked our mother what she remembered of the wait, and she said she remembered it like most remember pain: the hurt was white-hot at the time, practically blinding, but the memory would never reproduce the feeling. Like labor, or betrayal.

A FEW DAYS before your wedding, you and I went to the Buckhorn, a Petaluma dive. I'd invited your bride, too, though, sensing something, she'd politely declined.

You ordered a Coke and I had a whiskey because I could drink whatever I wanted by then.

Nervous?

Not too bad. A little.

And the bride?

She's excited, mostly.

That's good.

It was the first time that I actually longed not to be angry any-more. Finally I said: I've been trying to get pregnant, you know.

Oh? you said, and eyed my drink.

Tried, I corrected. I've tried to get pregnant.

Are you going to keep going?

I don't know.

Keep going, you said. I'd be a good uncle.

You're not surprised?

Surprised?

That I wanted to have kids?

You frowned and sipped on your Coke. Why would I be sur-prised? You're old and married. Isn't that what old married people do?

Then you said, Honestly, no, I'm not surprised. Mom told me you were having a hard time.

She did?

Yeah.

Recently?

Nah.

Oh, I said. Why didn't you say something then?

I don't know. Not really my business. Why didn't you?

I don't know, I said. I didn't know what you'd think.

If what?

If I decided to adopt.

I looked at you and said: What would you think? But what I didn't ask was what you would think if I didn't.

You laughed at the question, and for a moment the mood between us lightened. You were making it clear that, as usual, your sister was an idiot.

Obviously I would think it's a good idea, you said. What kind of stupid question is that?

I don't know, I said. I could feel my body beginning to betray me, cheeks pink, eyes down, legs crossed and recrossed in my chair. I was sorry for getting the question wrong.

Everything will be okay, you said finally, and this might sound schmaltzy, but you looked about ten years old again when you said it. I didn't start crying at the bar for that reason, for the sudden awareness of time passing so quickly, of the waste that the last year had been, with all the terrible things we'd said and all the true things we hadn't. I cried because when you said everything would be okay you meant it, that despite everything you still somehow never said things you didn't mean.

What did you get me for Christmas?

Not slippers.

You're just like Mom, you said, and I looked into your face to see how you meant it, but you were smiling. So emotional, you said. It's a wedding. Lighten up.

Right, I said.

Let's see if we can get something to eat here, you said, and I said, Cash only, and you patted your pockets to show you'd forgotten your wallet.

I'll pay, I said.

WAITING IS AN EXQUISITELY PRIVATE PAIN. It's the events that broadcast the joy and the grief, concrete losses and triumphs that a group can huddle around. But waiting we must do alone. We must wait for the sorrow to pass, for the memories to dull, for the hard work to pay off, for the object of our longing to arrive or depart. At my office one afternoon a woman confides in the bathroom that eventually her desire for a child just disappeared. The words wrap around me like wool, heating my neck and ears, and I wear them around for weeks, asking no one: Does a thing like that really just leave you?

Maybe this is how it leaves you: through the clomiphene citrate, the choriogonadotropin injections, the cod-liver oil, red raspberry leaf, nettle leaf, dandelion, red clover, vitamin Ds and Cs, folate, zinc, selenium, magnesium, anesthesia, progesterone creams, egg extractions, moderate exercise, ovulation kits, insulin regulation, thyroid stabilizers, sex with your legs straight up. The memories of how a house can hurt as much as a body, how long forgiveness in each can take.

IN READING OUR FATHER'S LETTERS again, I hear waiting. I read and reread them and hear a longing to get through the hour, the day, to leave, to see loved ones again, though he never says it, never once complains. I don't know anything about war, Danny; reading those letters did not help me understand it. But I realized this last time that they were written mostly for his mother, who probably needed to hear about the slow parts, the strangely happy parts, the day spent sitting around a bridge, or a beach. My guess is that the experience drilled an early understanding in that twenty-two-year-old boy, of loyalty, of duty, of protection, qualities shared between war and family. What I know from these letters is that there are many ways to say I love you, with words, with plain stories, or with the act of writing itself. What I know from our life is that he will never not come for you, for better or worse. *To the rescue.*

AND OUR MOTHER. Here is a woman who woke up in the dark every year on the morning of your birthday to decorate your doorway with streamers, who left notes in your lunches, who called the mother of every boy who bullied you. Here is a woman who offered up the hours to soccer games, science projects, school plays, who taught us which prayers to say when we were scared, or thankful, or had lost something. Here is a woman who asked us hard, direct questions because she wanted to know who we were, what mattered to us or worried us or thrilled us, who knew that despite any resistance we longed to be asked, to confess, to be known. Here is a woman who told us every chance she got that she loved being our mother. And here is a woman who never lived with the fear that your birth mother would come back for you, but did her best to navigate the absence, the second original sin.

Here is the only person on earth who has understood the weight and dimension of each loss and success. Who knew what it meant when you found a best friend, when you found a wife, when you graduated from college, left the mission trip. Who, whenever you strived after anything, did not warn of unreasonable expectations as I did, but who encouraged you, who said, And why shouldn't he be entitled to his ambition?

WHAT'S IT LIKE TO BE MARRIED, you'd asked me, and instead of answering with what everyone knows going in, I should have told you what I didn't, that the night before I got married I clung to our father, the night I went off the pill I clung to our mother, that all bright and ubiquitous changes in a life are always bound up in some kind of goodbye, some departure from one core unit to the next.

LIKE ANY MOTHER, real or imagined, ours contains a thousand lives that we'll never know. Only recently she told me that there were days in the beginning when she would go out to the shed and smoke. Later, when you were out of the house, when calls would come in about money, she'd sometimes return to the shed, though more often she found herself back at church, her prayers filling the empty pews. I don't think the experience was what she had expected; I don't think it fulfilled the visions that had stayed with her from St. Christopher's. Some days I don't think she felt like she was helping anybody by bringing you here, least of all you.

But these are only a mock-up of hard times, moments extracted from an entire life. What I know for certain is how much she loves you, how much she would have loved to hold you as an infant, to finish that paperwork sooner. But when the day came she dropped to her knees at the sight of you, took you into her arms, wrapped herself around the end of a long, tender wait. While all the anxieties of a new mother flooded in, she held you.

A T THE RECEPTION our parents and I work the room as if on the campaign trail. We exchange kind words with every cousin, aunt, uncle, and close family friend on your bride's side we can find; I escape to the bathroom only once to unzip the side of my dress and take a few deep breaths.

The location is a small hotel set on the water with dark wooden beams and vinyl flooring. Your guests collect around a large fireplace and under the tasteful white bulbs that have been strung from the ceiling. In the back corner a lone bartender serves beer, wine, and an insta-headache cocktail that the two of you crafted for the occasion. Each round table of six holds hydrangea and candles, and the windows surrounding the main room offer one last look at the water before the sun goes down.

On the wall by the dance floor, photos of the two of you are projected. This was your idea, of course. I had voted against it because slideshows like that seem reminiscent of the dead, each flashing image the length of a little life itself. But you'd insisted, so our mother and I collected old photos from the albums to be shown alongside the engagement photos with your bride. You appear as a three-foot Musketeer, then as a man in love, then again as a boy riding the teacups. I look over at your brother-in-law and he knows what I'm thinking: I'm still waiting for the moment to give you away. The site coordinator comes over and whispers in my ear.

AT THE LIBRARY last week I came across the line *I love thee with the passion put to use in my old griefs*, and for a moment I forgot about you and the speech. Lately I've been feeling something: not that I'm old but that I don't feel so young anymore. I remember when my husband and I first began trying for a child, how often I cried in our old apartments, about whether it was worth the time, the toll on my body, the grief. Soon it was a grief that loomed so large the whole world seemed to fit in it. Slowly, over time, after a very long wait, there came other kinds of days, days like today, where I look at you and your bride and notice again how big the world is, but not because it hurts any less.

What's it like to be married, you asked me. When I tell my husband that the line makes me think of him, that I love him with the passion put to use in my old griefs, he knows that it is both a kindness and a sadness. It's a sadness we're both ready to be free from, with the whole world stuck in such a small container, a house.

AFTER YOU CAME BACK from the mission trip, our mother pulled your Life Book from the shelf and brought it downstairs. She sat with you at the kitchen table and read it aloud and, for the first time, you listened to some of the beginning. *Not so long ago, a little boy was born in a faraway country. His name was Boon-Nam and this baby was you.* Our father came in from the garden and sat with you, too. You had some questions as she read, and they answered them. *We don't know what the woman who gave birth to you looked like, but we imagine that she must have been very beautiful. What do you think she looked like?* They told you again about your siblings.

They never wanted to associate those early years of your life with secrets or shame. In all the years on the shelf, a copy of your birth certificate rested inside that Life Book, the sole piece of paper that identified you as *Child No. 4*. They noticed this late and recalled Khun Preeda looking into our eyes and telling us that there were no siblings.

Again you nodded and took the news quietly. I don't know if this is information you'll pick up again later in life, or facts to be filed back on the shelf for good. I don't know if it's just become part of the family mythology given to us as children, the stories that follow us around forever. I don't know how these stories have served you growing up, but I've found that in my own life they've become the foundation. They were built to give you your place in the world, and helping to construct them has also given me mine.

RECENTLY I WENT TO A DISCUSSION GROUP in the city. There were about fifteen of us in the room; only three of the five panelists showed up. Based on the description, it was supposed to be a talk about adoption in contemporary literature. But it turned out no one cared about books; one woman raised her hand to tell her story about her daughter adopted from Guatemala, about how once walking through the streets, a young girl followed them for blocks saying, But why would you adopt her? Why? Why? Why? and then a panelist said, By definition adoption is a tragic thing, it starts as a tragedy, then another woman said, If I pick him up too quickly, people think he's getting abducted, then another woman, then another woman, and soon we were all sitting in a circle, talking over one another. It was mostly adoptive mothers there, a few adopted children, a few fathers. There were tears. I sat there listening. Even in all the reading I'd done, all the internet wormholes I'd traveled, I had still never heard people sit around and talk like this, about what it really felt like to be us.

After the discussion was over I stuck around, waited shyly to speak to one of the panelists. I had liked what she'd said about her son, whom she'd adopted as a toddler, and I told her so. Are you a mother? she asked. No, I whispered. I said a few things quickly and then she asked to exchange emails.

Later that evening, an email came through. It was just a pdf from the Child Welfare Information Gateway. I opened it and it said:

By three years of age, a baby's brain has reached almost 90 percent of its adult size. The growth in each region of the brain largely depends on receiving stimulation, which spurs activity, providing the foundation for learning. Just as positive experiences can assist with healthy brain development, experiences with maltreatment or neglect can negatively affect development, including changes to the structure and chemical activity of the brain and in the emotional and behavioral functioning of the child. The plasticity of the brain often allows children to recover from missing certain experiences, but it is likely to be more difficult.

The last page of the pdf showed a picture of two three-year-old brains held side by side, one marked as NORMAL and the other as EXTREME NEGLECT.

I looked at the picture and the old rage picked up in my chest, the instinct to defend you. I started a handful of responses about the problem with case studies, how they never filled in the full picture. Or the problem of anger or forgiveness or grief, how often they lacked a workable definition, or a clear explanation. Then instead of hitting send I shut my computer and turned out the light.

I turned the light back on, opened my computer. I looked at the picture again. It almost looked like a face, that three-year-old brain, and its frown was suddenly all I could see. It reminded me of a frown I used to love, a frown I still love, a frown that remains framed on my desk just out of the sunlight.

L AST NIGHT I told you that today might be hard for us, that you'd be all grown up, and of course there was more but that's where we stopped. I thanked you for asking me to speak, leaving out how difficult it was to speak to you, for you, about you, despite your bright portrait in our minds.

I wish I'd told you that there's so much possession wrapped up in love. Some days you don't see it or feel it at all, until something brings it into focus. Like that day you cut your head open at the basketball court and called me instead of our parents. I ran all the stop signs across town, double parked, sprinted to the group of boys circled around you, while you held a stranger's T-shirt to your face. We didn't know it was normal for a head wound to bleed so much, and I wondered if I might fail you and faint on the spot. And as you stared up at me, scared, waiting for my instruction, it was possession I felt as I ran to you, helped you up, put your arm around me, and led you back to my car. I talked you through that ride to the hospital, blood on the seat belt, blood on my shirt, my hand on your shoulder, and it wasn't until the boys had left your side mirror that you began to cry, shocked more by your fragility, I think, than your pain, and with each deep breath you took in to collect yourself I thought, mine, mine, mine.

Like that day on the court when I saw you for the first time since the mission trip, since the fight, since so long without speaking. You'd called and said, It's enough, I think we should see each other, and offered to come to my apartment, but I'd suggested there because it was a place where love always felt easy between us. You passed me the ball and we played under the hoop where we'd played as children, because words were no longer of use.

I wish I'd told you what my doctor had said, to see if you could walk me through it. She'd said, You have a few choices left, things that didn't really feel like choices at all.

I will be his parents one day, I told your brother-in-law once.

We will, he said.

YEARS AGO, when your brother-in-law moved to California from New York, I witnessed him say goodbye to his brother. They are shades of each other, as you know, one always mistaken for the other despite the years between them. We stood in the parking lot of an Italian restaurant, heading west in a U-Haul the next day, and I watched the two men cling to each other in a way that went beyond the boundaries of their bodies, like two twins fitted snugly in a womb. Their physical selves recognized each other up close, they recognized the oncoming danger, and they suddenly held on for dear life. A decision made biologically. I saw it from a distance and it shocked me. It shocked me to think of us, both ignorant to the recognition of a similar version of ourselves walking around in the world.

But that wasn't the case at all, because you had three siblings walking around somewhere. Three siblings plus me. And I will confess that I haven't known much jealousy in the decades that I've been your sister. I've hurt for you, worried for you, but rarely coveted. And the feeling reached me there on the concrete, thinking of your siblings. I was jealous of the three strangers you'd likely never know.

Recently, in a box full of paperwork, I found their names. They didn't live on any of the official documents, but instead on a single piece of Marriott stationery, given to our father on his return trip to Thailand two years following your adoption. He'd gone back to the orphanage and brought a white bear for each child, donated by a Sonoma County radio station, and standing once again in Khun Preeda's office, he watched her fill in the missing information from our last visit. The note is dated April 1996 and reads in careful handwriting: *Kamnan (18 years), Sunti (14 years), Dara (11 years)*.

This is what I mean about love: in the wild possession I felt when I saw their names, the youngest sister exactly my age. And though our parents have told you all this, I put the paper back and closed the box like a secret, because I wanted you to belong to me alone.

THERE HAVE BEEN TIMES over the course of your life—when our parents have gone traveling, when you brought your wife over to the apartment—when the room has quieted and I've held binoculars up to the future, visions that flutter in and out as quickly as the birds, and I've glimpsed the day when we both become orphans. I have tried to taxonomize the ways you will need me. At night in bed while my husband sleeps soundly, I do not hear *Who am I? Who am I?*, words that would so often call out to me as a girl. Instead I think: What is a mother? I have only ever had that one to go on, one who is so impressive to me, so full of grace that any comparison to myself feels ridiculous. I think of how I have loved you and failed you. I think of how I have lost us to our stories. Have I stolen your life, your dignity, for the sake of mythology? Of self-preservation? Perhaps I haven't grown up at all.

And yet. When I think of the way I love you, how I have built you a roof with my love, thatched thick by careful hands, I consider the way it stands firm even when the world shakes. It is my nature to shoo you under at the first sign of trouble, simple as holding you, as breathing; it is my nature to ensure your protection.

And I know that you, too, loved me immediately from the beginning, despite my pale skin, and Mom's ears, and Dad's hair, and for this I will be forever grateful.

Then it's my turn to stand up and speak.

I DO NOT SAY: Not so long ago, a little boy was born in a faraway country. His name was Boon-Nam and this baby was you. The woman who gave birth to you knew that she could not give you all the things you needed, and so you came to us. Or rather, we came to you.

I do not say that many years later you told us you were ready to return to that faraway country. We said we'd join you but you wanted to do it on your own. We felt the kind of puncture in our heart and shins akin to growing pains, except by then you were already grown. So we helped you plan the trip and sent you on your way. It seemed like the story should end there and, very briefly, it did.

I do not say that broken hearts are so wearisome to carry around, because I don't have to tell you that. I understand why you're quick to put it all behind you, to do your best to forget once the anger subsides.

I do not say that everyone carries their own narrative of the world in their head. We're made most human by these visions, in how limited or expansive a life's story can become, the conviction with which we believe things should or might or did happen, and in all the ways we get it wrong. I had visions of your return to the Babies' Home; I saw you walking the halls, eyeing the beds and the floors and the children with the same kind of scrutiny and care as we once had, the images branded there mostly forever. I could see you so clearly as you drifted down the canal on that boat. But you never made it to any of the places traced in my dreams, close as you were, and I realize now that maybe you never will.

I do not say that it's an impossible task, trying to fit you on a page. To describe how much I love you, how my love for you works. Like a tantrum or a firework, a dizzying ride in a teacup. Like an old, intimate joke that through the decades keeps its punch line, though nobody can remember how it started.

I do not say that I still can't answer how our story should be kept or told, how it falls in or out with history's long catalog of wounds and tropes. I have only come to this: meeting you that day all those years ago became the axis on which everything else has spun.

WHEN THE TWO OF US WERE STILL CHILDREN, I used to imagine your birth mother looking down on me every time I was tough on you. It scared me to consider what she might be thinking, if she was happy with the results of your life. Imagining her up there would often put me on better behavior, for a few minutes at least.

Now I look at you with your suit, your wife, and I say goodbye to old fears and welcome in new ones. I try to speak for our mother and father who love you so dearly, but mostly of course I speak for myself. You asked me just the other day if you could still come home as often after getting married, now that you were all grown up. There is so much I cannot tell you about the future, Danny. But I'll be there to open the door, to hang up your jacket; I'll be there to welcome you in.

ACKNOWLEDGMENTS

It's a long road toward a first book. Thank you to Sarah Bowlin for being the first to believe in this project and for shepherding it through every stage with wisdom and care. To Emily Bell, for your brilliant editorial vision. To Jackson Howard, Chandra Wohleber, Alexis Nowicki, Abby Kagan, and the entire team at FSG, and to Thomas Colligan for the beautiful cover design. To Željka Marošević, for being such a sharp and thoughtful editor and for sending me the metallic tote bag of my dreams.

I'm forever grateful to the graduate program at Columbia University and the Clein-Lemann Esperanza Fellowship. Thank you to the writing program at San Francisco State and the generous people behind the Bambi Holmes Award. Special thanks to Matthew Clark Davison for your mentorship during that time.

To Anthony Marra, Julie Buntin, and Rachel Khong for your early support.

To Lizzie Harris, for being as generous a reader as you are a person, and to Andrew Eisenman, for many years of friendship and for introducing me to Lizzie.

To Kate Cornell, who taught me so much in the hours spent away from this book, and to Eustacio Humphrey.

To my California and New York families and friends, whose love has been my lifeline. To Uncle Ron, avid reader, who helped me at a time when I needed it most.

To my parents and my brother, whose love has guided me my entire life, and whom I love with more words than can fill a book. And to my dear sister.

To Samuel, for the insane happiness you have brought to all of us.

And to Adam, who has been with this project since before the beginning, who read hundreds of drafts with patience and intelligence, whose opinion I value most of all. Without you, none of this.

A Note About the Author

Ashley Nelson Levy received her MFA from Columbia University, where she was awarded the Clein-Lemann Esperanza Fellowship. Her work has received a notable mention in *The Best American Nonrequired Reading*, and she is a recipient of the Bambi Holmes Award for Emerging Writers. In 2015, she cofounded Transit Books, an independent publishing house with a focus on international literature. This is her first book.